"I've Reach___
My Patience, Diana."

He began to pull her closer, and she felt herself shiver. She couldn't allow him to intimidate her with his anger, she couldn't! Pushing frantically against his chest, she lifted a face filled with remorse.

"Don't you understand?" she whispered, shaking her head in defeat. "How else can I fight the way you make me feel? It's wrong, Josh. I won't sacrifice myself . . . not even for you."

"I don't want a sacrifice," he murmured, his tongue gently tracing her lips until she wanted to scream with frustrated desire. "I'm asking for a gift."

NICOLE MONET

is an inveterate writer of romances who lives in California with her husband and daughter. Writing is her full-time career. "I write," the author says, "because I am a voracious reader, and I feel that in some small way, I'm paying back all the pleasure I've received in my lifetime."

Dear Reader:

SILHOUETTE DESIRE is an exciting new line of contemporary romances from Silhouette Books. During the past year, many Silhouette readers have written in telling us what other types of stories they'd like to read from Silhouette, and we've kept these comments and suggestions in mind in developing SILHOUETTE DESIRE.

DESIREs feature all of the elements you like to see in a romance, plus a more sensual, provocative story. So if you want to experience all the excitement, passion and joy of falling in love, then SILHOUETTE DESIRE is for you.

I hope you enjoy this book and all the wonderful stories to come from SILHOUETTE DESIRE. I'd appreciate any thoughts you'd like to share with us on new SILHOUETTE DESIRE, and I invite you to write to us at the address below:

Karen Solem
Editor-in-Chief
Silhouette Books
P.O. Box 769
New York, N.Y. 10019

NICOLE MONET
Shadow Of Betrayal

Silhouette Desire

Published by Silhouette Books New York

America's Publisher of Contemporary Romance

Other Silhouette Books by Nicole Monet

Love's Silver Web

SILHOUETTE BOOKS, a Simon & Schuster Division of
GULF & WESTERN CORPORATION
1230 Avenue of the Americas, New York, N.Y. 10020

ISBN: 0-671-45860-4

First Silhouette Books printing January, 1983

10 9 8 7 6 5 4 3 2 1

America's Publisher of Contemporary Romance

Printed in the U.S.A.

Shadow Of
Betrayal

1

As she pegged the last sheet onto the clothesline, Diana Moreland wondered how she kept functioning, when all she could think about was the letter that had been waiting for her when she returned home from work yesterday. It was from some law firm she had never even heard of before today.

The crumpled sheet was still there on her desk where she had flung it. She remembered the gradual stiffening of her body as she read the intimidating document, and the panic which had caused it.

He was coming here! The wind sighing through the tall trees shading the yard seemed to echo the words. With troubled eyes she glanced toward the rustling branches, her gaze settling on the small boy playing beneath them.

At two and a half, Steven was big for his age, but his

sturdy frame in masculine jeans and a windbreaker appeared absurdly vulnerable to Diana's loving eyes.

Becoming aware of her scrutiny, Steven looked up, a big grin lighting his face as he called to her.

"Mama, come see!"

With a lump in her throat she approached the pile of damp leaves and bracken. "That's a wonderful mountain, darling. I believe that's the best one you've ever made."

Making mountains out of anything and everything was Steven's newest craze. He had a lively, inventive mind and was never happier than when he was turning his ideas into reality. At least this newest obsession was relatively harmless, she thought, unless you counted dinner last night. She had certainly objected to the mountain he had built with his mashed potatoes!

Still, that was nothing compared to the problem his painting had caused. Last month he had become fascinated with painting dots. That in itself had seemed an innocuous activity, until he decided that their weathered hardwood floors would look much prettier if embellished a little.

She managed to remove the paint without too much difficulty. It wasn't Steven's fault that she had also lifted ninety percent of the varnish. That had been a rather expensive cleanup job, she thought, grimacing.

After admonishing Steven to remain where he was, she moved slowly up the slight incline toward the back door of the small house they had shared since Steven was just a couple of months old. It was more of a vacation cabin, really, but it was all they had ever needed.

Single-storied and made of weathered knotty pine, it was situated far enough back from the main road so as to give the little house an aura of isolation, nestled within its own sunlit grove of spruce, pine, and eucalyptus trees. She had fallen in love with it on sight. The serene, storybook quality of the house and its setting appealed to the lonely, grief-stricken young woman she had been then. With a sudden frown creasing the smoothness of her brow, she wondered if she had ever been free of grief.

Entering the screened-in porch, which had been converted into a combination laundry room and play area, she began to fold the small garments she took from the dryer. She wished she had the time to line-dry Steven's clothes, but usually satisfied herself with the knowledge that at least his bedding had the fresh scent of sunlight and pine.

Steven! Everything she did, every thought she had, revolved around him. He was all the family she had left, and she would fight for him with the last breath in her body. If that man thought he could come here and pick up the last little piece of his disastrous relationship with Joanna, he had a big surprise in store!

He had deserted his wife when she needed him most. Surely the law would uphold her claim to her sister's child, would take into consideration Josh's failure to accept responsibility for Steven even before his birth. As soon as her mind formulated the thought she feared the answer, and cold panic gripped her.

A derisive smile curved her lips as she remembered the persuasive personality of Joshua Cambridge. What chance would she have to convince the court to find in her favor? Even five years ago he had projected a confident self-assurance. She had sensed a kindness and sensitivity that she later discovered to be illusions, and she knew, with a sense of doom, that she stood little or no chance of convincing a judge that Joshua Cambridge was other than the man he seemed.

Josh would have no difficulty portraying the image of an anguished father, she thought with unusual cynicism. He was a writer and, as such, a keen observer of human nature. She recalled vividly how sickened she had been when, shortly after Joanna's death, his first novel was acclaimed as having "rare insight into the human heart" and "unusual sensitivity." She had wanted to rip to shreds the reviewers and newscasters who fawned over this newest light on their horizon. Why should he enjoy the best of life, she recalled thinking, while Joanna lay dead?

Carrying Steven's clothes through to the tiny cubbyhole that served as his bedroom, she prayed silently for the strength to somehow get through the next hours until his arrival. In the letter, Josh's lawyer referred to his client as Steven's father, but in no way would she give credence to such a claim!

Her hands shook as they carefully placed the small garments in appropriate drawers. No matter how much she personally might deny it, according to the lawyer there was no doubt about the validity of the man's right to be considered the legal parent. He had sent her a copy of Joanna's marriage certificate, informing her that although separated at the time of Steven's birth, his parents were still legally man and wife. The legalities were all so cut and dried, she thought, anger foremost in her mind. Did no one care about the love a small boy felt for the only person in his life he had ever called "Mama"?

Glancing at the watch adorning her wrist, she gasped. If she didn't get a move on she would be late opening the preschool. She had planned on arriving earlier than usual, to give herself a chance to go over the books in relative peace and quiet, and today of all days she knew she needed the mechanical comfort of following a normal routine.

As she hurried through her shower and later dressed in warm, corded slacks of sable-brown, topped by a matching brown and gold pullover sweater, she deliberately cleared her mind of anything but the tasks at hand.

Getting Steven cleaned up and in the car within the limits of the time she allotted herself was no easy task, but she accomplished it with a few minutes to spare. With the heater turned on full blast she maneuvered the car down the bumpy graveled side road that served as their driveway, stopping briefly to check the traffic before pulling out onto the main thoroughfare.

She drove slowly, absently listening to Steven's chatter as they negotiated the short distance to the school. She was so much luckier than most working mothers with small children, because she could have Steven with her during her working hours. Since she was part owner of the school, there was no one to object to his presence.

She and her friend Elaine, who was more like a mother than anything else, had started the Singing Chimes Preschool just over a year ago. She had wanted to escape from the memories Los Angeles held for her, and after vacationing in Tahoe, she and Elaine had decided that Tahoe was the perfect place for the preschool they had been wanting to open.

That first year hadn't been easy, but they managed to survive until the school began to show a profit. Elaine put her life savings into the venture, and Diana had used nearly all of the small legacy left to her by her parents.

They had met when Diana was fresh out of college, the proud possessor of her teacher's certificate, which told the world she was a qualified nursery-school instructor. Elaine was the person who interviewed her for her first job at a privately funded parochial preschool in Los Angeles.

She had been everywhere seeking employment, discovering to her dismay that excellent qualifications weren't the open sesame she imagined. The one qualification she didn't possess was experience. Since she couldn't get that unless someone hired her, she was more than slightly on the defensive when she finally sat in front of Elaine's gentle countenance.

Elaine had guided the interview skillfully, and it was only much later, when her first elation over securing the position faded, that Diana realized just how much of herself she had shown to the other woman. Somehow Elaine had managed to draw her out until she laughed and chatted unself-consciously. During that interview Elaine discovered Diana's love for children and the deep need she herself had to love and be loved.

It hadn't taken many weeks of working together before Elaine knew of Diana's upbringing, and the emotional insecurity that had resulted from having to constantly earn her parents' approval. She could talk to Elaine as she had never been able to talk to her mother, but still she had been shocked when she found herself divulging her innermost fear to her friend. It was something she tried to keep hidden, even from herself, and Elaine's shaken response had burst open the dam behind which Diana's emotions had been contained.

"What do you mean, you're not the kind of woman that generates lasting love in a man?" Elaine exclaimed. "You're beautiful, intelligent, and what's more important, you've a wealth of loving inside you, just waiting for the right man to tap its sweetness."

It had all come out then, all the anguish and torment she had suffered because of her fiancé's defection. She had been so certain of Gilbert's love, until she saw the look on his face the first time he met Joanna. That had been the beginning of the end for them, and she had never completely recovered from a sense of inadequacy regarding her own attractiveness and femininity.

Although the wound inflicted by Gilbert remained, somehow sharing her bitterness with her friend had cauterized the festering in her soul. Elaine, bless her, hadn't hesitated to give both affection and support which gradually succeeded in building Diana's confidence and awareness of her own potential. It was only during unguarded moments like this that the past returned to haunt her, she mused.

"Steven, don't you dare try to get out of that car seat. You know what I told you the last time."

The admonishment, accompanied by a warning frown that Steven countered with an unrepentant grin, was automatic, but succeeded in diverting her attention from her thoughts. Noticing for the first time the brilliance of the blue sky, Diana rolled down her window a crack, breathing deeply of the musky sweetness of dripping foliage.

Snow still lay on the trees and roadside, although the early approach of spring was taking its toll. Although she loved the sight of the snow-laden countryside, Diana admitted feeling a preference for warmth and sunshine. It wasn't easy keeping children amused indoors for over ten hours, when the falling snow promised untold delights.

Preschoolers were naturally intrepid little people, who didn't understand the difference between the words "snow" and "storm." The falling white drifts, which carried an icy wind and obscured visibility, seemed the greatest fun, and they became fractious and irritable at restrictions which to them seemed incomprehensible. Diana chuckled as she remembered some of the antics she and Elaine had been reduced to performing for their amusement.

They were turning into the circular driveway of the converted house that served as the school. Shutting off the engine, she set the emergency brake and turned to hug the child at her side.

"Here we are, darling!"

A small snub nose spattered with freckles wrinkled engagingly, while carroty curls nestled momentarily at her throat.

Pulling the fur-lined hood of Steven's windbreaker up over his head, Diana removed the safety harness he found so irksome and lifted him from the car. As she walked toward the school's entrance Steven was a heavy but welcome weight in her arms. Lowering him onto the weathered boards of the porch that fronted the building, she quickly unlocked the door and ushered him inside. As she watched him happily toddle off, her mouth was set with grim determination. The threat hanging over their heads from Joshua Cambridge would be faced, somehow. The only thing she was sure of, without any doubt, was her own tenacity.

She was the only mother Steven had ever known, and she had earned the right to keep him. If Josh thought he could calmly enter their lives and take him from her, he could think again. Josh, in her estimation, had long ago forfeited any rights to his son by his cruelty to the boy's mother.

Leaving Steven drawing contentedly at the long table set against the far wall, Diana moved to turn on the heater. The blast of warm air from the vent was welcome, and she stood for a moment warming her hands. Coats would remain on until the room had had the chance to warm, she decided, walking toward the corner desk she shared with Elaine.

Withdrawing the folder containing their budget for the month, she began making computations with the ease of long practice. A frown furrowed her forehead as she concentrated on making their money stretch to include some new play equipment they were talking of buying.

No matter how many times she added the columns, she realized, the result would be the same. Unless they took on more children, there just wouldn't be enough left over after paying bills and buying food for the hot lunches they provided. Throwing down the pencil in disgust, she rubbed her temples to ease the slight pounding she could feel building in her head and sighed. Now was not the time to worry about finances. Her mind was too preoccupied with the added strain in her personal life to worry about something as frivolous as swing sets!

Cold air fanned her back, and she turned to smile at Elaine as she stood framed in the doorway.

"Brrr," Elaine growled, hurriedly closing the door behind her. "Looks like we're due for one of those March storms we've been anticipating."

"Your old bones just can't take the cold," Diana teased, getting to her feet and hanging her own coat on the wall rack beside the desk. "How can you predict a storm when the sky is cloudless."

"Are you kidding?" Elaine gasped, pointing her finger at the curtained window. "You must have driven to work in a fog, my girl. If those aren't storm clouds, I'd like to know what they are!"

Walking to the window, Diana pulled back the curtains, her brow creasing in dismay. Just an hour before, the heavens had been a clear and unobstructed blue; now angry masses obscured the sun. With a sigh of resignation she turned, frowning in disgust.

"That's all I needed to make today perfect," she protested, rubbing the back of her neck in a tired motion.

Hanging up her coat and scarf, Elaine turned to study Diana's strained features, her own forming into an expression of concern.

"What gives, honey? It isn't just the weather that's got you down, that's for sure."

16

Biting her lip while looking in Steven's direction, she motioned for Elaine to follow her out of the room into their small, but compact, kitchen. While making coffee, Diana unburdened herself. Elaine, ever tactful, made no attempt to interrupt the rather incoherent flow of words, and waited until they were both seated at the table with their cups before attempting to make some sense out of her friend's ramblings.

"Did the letter say exactly when he would arrive?" she questioned, holding on to her own calm with difficulty.

"Today," Diana admitted, briefly closing her eyes and leaning back against the chair. "Shock tactics to throw me off guard, wouldn't you say? At least, according to the lawyer, Josh will have the decency to call and set up a time to see Steven. That was a wise move on his part." Her lip curled derisively. "If he just presented himself at our front door, I'd probably slam it in his face!"

Listening intently, Elaine thought of the agony in store for Diana, as well as for herself. Diana was like a daughter to her, and Steven was her joy, the grandson she had never expected to have. If the boy's father succeeded in gaining custody, what would they do?

As if she had read her friend's mind, Diana cried, "Elaine, what am I going to do?"

Elaine didn't respond to the question immediately, and took the time to raise the coffee mug to her lips before replying. She needed to be strong enough to help Diana, and she wouldn't achieve that by allowing her own panic to show.

"Honey, all you can do is just wait until he arrives.

I'm sure he's a reasonable man, who'll be compassionate enough to understand your position."

"Reasonable?" Diana muttered. "Was it a reasonable man who tormented Joanna into leaving her home with hardly a cent to her name? He knew she was pregnant and wouldn't be able to support herself by going back to modeling. You know the condition she was in when she finally managed to reach me in Los Angeles. Six months pregnant and gray with fatigue. The things she told us about her husband belonged in a horror story, not real life, and I'm damned if a man like that is going to get my baby!"

Yes! she thought. Steven was her child, earned through the agony she had shared with her sister when he was born. Her memory of the night Joanna had given him birth was still as vivid as ever, and she shuddered as her mind traveled the familiar path.

Her hands had damply clutched the steering wheel, her eyes trying to pierce the thick fog. She heard Joanna's screaming moans, which eventually faded to pained whimpers, every sound seeming to pierce her own body.

"It won't be long now, Joanna. Everything will be all right."

"It won't!" The protest was accompanied by a violent jerk of Joanna's body. "After what happened, nothing will ever be right again. Oh, Diana," she gasped, as another contraction seized her. "I'm going to die. I never wanted this baby, and now I'm to be punished for my sins. J-Josh would ha-have been happy."

"That's nonsense, and you know it," she comforted, while her own mind seethed with doubts. The man's a monster, she thought. That Joanna saw her husband as capable of enjoying his wife's torment was incomprehensible to her. Surely there had been reason for the hysterical certainty in her sister's voice? Even now, so many months later, she was still tormented by the question.

Leaning back in her chair, Elaine met Diana's eyes with unswerving purpose. Reminded of Joanna's bitterness and hate, her almost unbalanced loathing of the tangible evidence of her pregnancy during the last months of her life, Elaine couldn't help wondering just how much truth there had been in her vitriolic words.

At the time of Steven's birth, Diana had been nearly incoherent with grief over the death of her sister and had become hysterical when Elaine suggested contacting the baby's father. That was the closest they had ever come to an argument, Elaine remembered. Still, if she was to be the kind of friend Diana needed at this moment, she knew she had to break the long silence she had imposed on herself where Joanna was concerned.

"What are you thinking?" Diana asked the question with trepidation, not liking the hardened expression on Elaine's normally cheerful face.

Before replying, Elaine drew a deep breath. She had lowered her eyes to the mug cradled against wrinkled hands, but now she again forced herself to look up.

"You said that Joanna's life with her husband belonged in a horror story. Don't you think it possible, considering her mental condition at the time, that she might have embellished the truth. You knew your sister better than I did, but I'll say now what I thought then.

Everyone deserves the chance to defend themselves against character-destroying accusations of that sort, and Joshua Cambridge is no exception!"

"How can you even consider listening to the man who literally destroyed his wife?" Diana gasped, shaking her head in repudiation while she glared accusingly in Elaine's direction. "The Joanna you knew was a parody of the real person, Elaine. I know she was demanding and resentful during her pregnancy, but after what she'd been through, is it so surprising? She was so beautiful before her marriage, her lips full and unmarred by discontent, her hair a glorious titian worn like a crown. When I saw her standing at the door, ill and unkempt, and discovered the reason for her condition, I wanted to kill Joshua Cambridge!"

"Is that why you lied to the authorities? Was it your way of righting the wrong you felt had been done to your sister, by depriving Joshua Cambridge of his son? Or was there more to it, Diana? By helping your sister to revenge herself, were you also striking a blow against all men, because of what Gilbert did to you?"

Diana's face whitened at the accusation, her eyes enormous. "You know that's not true," she whispered, fighting against the tears threatening to fall. "I did what Joanna had asked me to do. For the love of God, Elaine . . . it was her dying wish!"

Sudden contrition glistened in Elaine's eyes for the pain she was causing her friend, but she knew she had to harden herself in order to make Diana see both sides of this situation. Although she had known Joanna for only a few months, it had taken Elaine only minutes to see through the facade, which Joanna maintained in Diana's presence, to the selfish, vain creature behind it.

Taking a firm grip on Diana's shaking hand, Elaine leaned forward to better emphasize her next words.

"I'm sorry, honey," she whispered, strengthening the force of her grip. "You know I don't want to hurt you; you've been through enough pain without my adding to your troubles. But Diana, you can't approach Steven's father with this bitterness eating at your insides. Give the man a chance to tell his side of the story. Otherwise you might lose Steven altogether. Have you taken time to realize that if Joshua Cambridge gains custody of Steven, he could take him away from here and deny you all access to him?"

Diana remained silent, the antipathy engendered by Elaine's words causing her to bite down hard on her lower lip. Surely such a thing could never happen! The thought was totally unacceptable!

"I'm not asking you to believe ill of your own sister, but for Steven's sake as well as your own, I'm begging you to tread softly where Joshua Cambridge is concerned." Elaine rose to her feet, giving Diana a consoling hug before she turned to answer the persistent knocking at the front door.

Diana spent the rest of the day engaged in her normal routine. She led the children in learning songs, supervised their drawing, and yet felt herself strangely dissociated from the noisy activity around her. Her mind kept going over and over her conversation with Elaine, and at the end of the long and frustrating day, she didn't like the conclusion she had drawn.

Was it possible that Elaine might be right in her conjectures? Had she subconsciously been too ready to believe the worst of Josh because of her own bitterness over the past? Even if her motives had been the purest, she had had no right to play judge and jury, she thought. By keeping silent about the existence of Steven's father, didn't you yourself commit what amounts to a crime? her conscience added with a sneer.

She had tried! she consoled herself. When Joanna first informed her that she planned on having the baby under her maiden name, hadn't she remonstrated with her? Hadn't she tried to convince her that what she proposed to do wasn't fair to the child, let alone herself? Yes, the nagging little voice inside whispered, but even though you knew Joanna incapable of making a rational judgment, you still went along with it. And what was worse, the voice continued, after Joanna's death you made no attempt to let Josh know of his son's existence.

She had tried to justify her decision to remain silent by telling herself she was following through on her sister's last wishes, but was that true? she wondered. Could Elaine be right in thinking her silence was caused by an irrational desire for revenge, or had she been determined to keep the child she had loved on sight entirely to herself, regardless of whether or not she had the moral right to do so?

She was never more glad to reach the snug security of their home than she was that night. The only good thing about the long and exhausting day was the talk she had initiated with Elaine before they left the school. She promised her friend to consider her advice carefully, and the rush of tears Elaine shed erased the unaccustomed strain between them.

After a substantial but uninspiring meal, Diana played quietly with Steven on the rug in front of the fire. She was bone-tired, but wouldn't even consider putting him to bed earlier than usual. She was savoring the precious minutes with him, but eventually Steven's drooping eyelids silently protested the lateness of the hour.

Carrying him into her room, she had him giggling delightedly as she told him nonsense rhymes. After she had changed into a pair of comfortably aged lounging pajamas of turquoise satin, she ushered him into the bathroom, anticipation of the nighttime ritual lightening her mood.

The actual bathing and washing of hair took only minutes, but as usual Steven wasn't content with that. Splashing frenetically, until Diana was nearly as wet as he, he demanded his boats, grinning up at her with good-natured determination.

"All right, you little stinker." She laughed, dropping a kiss on his nose. "I'll let you play for five minutes longer, but only if you promise not to get any more water on the floor."

Steven's method of answering was to slap the water excitedly with his hands, soaking both the floor and the laughing woman kneeling beside the tub. Reaching inside the cabinet underneath the sink, she handed him two small windup boats. While he played and made all the appropriate sounds, she began mopping up the evidence of his enjoyment.

With that task accomplished, she lifted Steven from

the now cooling water. Wrapping him in a large, fluffy towel, she held him up to the mirror so he could see his reflection.

She smiled, hugging his sweet-smelling body closely against her. "Now that we've gotten the dirt off, aren't you a pretty fellow?"

"Mama's pretty," he giggled, patting her cheek with a chubby hand.

"You're a charmer, all right. Now, let's get you into pajamas and I'll tell you a story before you go to sleep. What'll it be tonight?" she questioned, knowing very well the answer she would receive.

"Big-boy story!"

"All right." She laughed, bouncing him up and down in her arms as they headed in the direction of his bedroom. "A big-boy story it is."

She couldn't remember why she had started telling Steven stories about a little boy with red hair who went to sleep at night and was magically transformed by the sandman into a big boy who had marvelous adventures. Now she doubted that she could get him to sleep without the nightly ritual, but she didn't mind. She enjoyed making up the outlandish tales as much as Steven enjoyed hearing them.

Tonight, though, the hero had only gone as far as the top of the mountain before his smaller counterpart was fast asleep. Placing a last kiss on the back of his head and patting his raised bottom lovingly, she turned down the shaded racing-car lamp until only the night-light was burning.

Leaving the door opened a crack, Diana walked down the cramped hallway, intending to turn out the lights in the living room before seeking the comfort of her own bed. The sound of the phone ringing on the hall stand caused her to jump nervously, and her fingers trembled as she reached for the receiver.

She knew, even before she lifted the phone from its cradle, that it would be Josh. This intuition quickened the blood in her veins, causing her to hestitate idiotically while stating her name.

The voice at the other end of the line was one she thought she had forgotten, but her reaction to the deep masculine tones made a fallacy of that supposition. There was a weight pressing against her chest as she struggled to breathe, a roaring in her ears that no amount of self-loathing would eliminate.

"I . . . I agree that this isn't the best way to talk after all this time, Josh," she stammered, her fingers icy cold as they worried the cord she clutched nervously. "When and where do you suggest we meet?"

2

~~~~~~~~~~~~~~~~~

Diana paced the floor of the recreation room that was part of the plush lakeshore condominium unit where Joshua Cambridge was staying. For what seemed the thousandth time she turned to Steven, who sat contentedly watching one of his favorite television programs on a five-foot screen.

Knowing immediately the area he described, Diana hadn't had any difficulty following Josh's directions. She had long admired the architectural perfection of the buildings that blended so well with the natural beauty of their setting; yet now that she was here, waiting for him to arrive, her heart nearly overflowing with dread, she found little comfort in the luxury of her surroundings.

They had passed tennis courts on their way in, as well as an Olympic-size swimming pool, and her momentary twinge of envy of the man lucky enough to inhabit these surroundings sickened her. She didn't want to admire anything about Joshua Cambridge, not even the place he chose to make a temporary residence.

Remembering their brief, stilted phone conversation of the night before caused gooseflesh to rise on her arms. There had been suppressed violence underlying the stiff politeness of his voice, she was sure of it! Was this confidence-stripping wait he was making her endure some subtle kind of torture? she wondered, anger beginning to take the edge off her nervousness. Crossing her arms across her chest, she grimaced at the sight of the snow falling steadily outside. Was it her imagination, or was the storm that had finally broken loose just an hour ago worsening? She suddenly felt trapped, and she didn't like the feeling. If Josh didn't get here in another five minutes, she would collect Steven and return home, she promised herself, prior arrangement be damned.

A man's voice sounded just behind her, and she jumped as though she had been shot. Feeling almost faint from the effects of her tension, she turned, her pupils dilating until she seemed all eyes to the contrite man standing before her.

"I'm sorry, my dear," he apologized, a rueful grin adding even more creases to the roundness of his face. Smoothing back nonexistent hair from the top of a shiny bald head with one hand, he offered his other hand in greeting.

"I'm Charles Evans, the manager of this humble establishment," he said, his eyes twinkling as he gestured expansively. "Mr. Cambridge has asked me to arrange for a car to take you to his place, Mrs. Moreland."

She didn't attempt to correct Mr. Evans's assumption that she was married. All of her friends here in Tahoe had naturally assumed that she was a widow or divorcée. Because she and Steven looked so much alike, they never considered that he might not be her son, so she was used to being called Mrs. Moreland.

Diana's instant liking for the man she faced showed in the sweetness of her smile, which gave her face a loveliness of which she was quite unaware.

"Please call him back and tell him that I would rather our meeting take place here, Mr. Evans. M-my little boy is quite content at the moment, and I would rather not take him out in this weather any more than I have to," she explained, her trepidation apparent in the tense carriage of her head.

"The name's Curly," he admonished, smiling widely to try to bring a return expression that had almost taken his breath away only moments before. When Diana stared at him pleadingly, biting her bottom lip, his smile faded and his face creased in concern. "You won't have to worry about your little fella going out in this snowfall, Mrs. Moreland. Mr. Cambridge's unit is only about half a mile down the road, and he's ordered one of our staff cars to take you there."

She was being railroaded into an intimacy she would rather avoid, but she didn't want to make a scene by refusing to follow Mr. Evans from the room, so she had little choice but to move with him to the waiting sedan.

Thanking Mr. Evans for his trouble, she put a disgruntled Steven, who had had to be dragged from his television program, into the car and slid in beside him. She snuggled the child against her and tried to subdue the foreboding she felt as she noticed the increasing ferocity of the falling snow. Well, she consoled herself. At least she would have a good excuse for cutting their so-called visit short!

The minimal distance they traveled gave Diana little chance to gain control over her nervousness. It had been bad enough waiting for their meeting in the impersonal atmosphere of the condominium's clubhouse, but at least she had had the comfort of other people around her. How much more trying this whole situation was going to be now that there would be just the three of them in the intimacy of Josh's home.

The driver obligingly carried Steven to the imposing double doors of the condominium unit, and Diana watched his departure with the sensation of having lost her best friend. Taking a deep breath of the frosty air, and clutching Steven's hand as she would a lifeline, she lifted her hand to an ornate brass knocker.

She wasn't prepared to have the wooden panels open almost immediately and had to suppress a gasp at the sight of the man she had hoped never to see again. He was larger, more imposing than she remembered, but every bit as devastating. She had forgotten the massive width of his shoulders and chest, which tapered down to lean hips and muscled thighs, and the way artificial light turned the gold of his hair to streaked silver.

Swallowing with difficulty, she finally found the courage to raise her eyes to his face. A shocked exclamation almost forced itself from between her lips, which she nervously moistened with the tip of her tongue. The eyes that studied her so closely were as blue as she remembered, but surely they had never been so coldly condemning? She quavered inwardly.

If Diana found herself surprised at the appearance of the man now silently ushering them through the doorway, that was nothing to the impact she made on Joshua Cambridge. As Diana came forward into the light of the entry hall he nearly choked on a swiftly indrawn breath.

The woman facing him, defiance in the taut lines of her body, was a far cry from the shy, easily intimidated girl he used to know. As their eyes locked together he felt a tremor shake him.

At that moment Steven, frightened by this huge stranger, hid his head in the folds of Diana's woolen jumper and uttered a whimper of protest. Immediately Diana knelt, offering the child little murmurs of encouragement and comfort. With shaking hands she pulled back the hood of his parka, and Joshua Cambridge found himself staring at his son for the first time.

His heart caught at the boy's similarity to the face so close to his, but the resemblance wasn't to be wondered at, he thought, a steel fist clutching at his heart. He had known, of course, how much alike the two sisters had been, but as he studied the features of the boy and his aunt, he felt an unpleasant sense of shock. The boy was the image of his mother, nothing in the tiny features of the man who had fathered him.

Despair was a leaden weight in his chest, until Steven

chose that moment to look upward. Smoky blue eyes met their counterpart, the child's reflecting shyness, while the man's held the dawning of joyous recognition. He has my eyes! he thought, his throat tightening with emotion.

His thoughts twisted torturously backward, to the time he had first discovered his son's existence. For the better part of a year his lawyer had been trying to trace Joanna in order to start divorce proceedings. Josh had never suspected, the day he entered the lawyer's office for a hastily arranged conference, the nature of the information about to be given.

By the time he finally stumbled from the room, his appearance caused the normally impersonal expression of his lawyer's secretary to change to one of concern.

"Are you all right, Mr. Cambridge?"

He stared at her mutely, his legs automatically carrying him from the outer office. Once in the hall his control broke, and he slumped shakily against the wall.

Dead! Joanna was dead, and the child that had extinguished the vibrant flame of her life was very much alive and being cared for by his aunt. How ironic that Joanna, who had hated the thought of distorting her body by pregnancy, had in the end presented him with the one thing for which he had hungered. A terrible guilt assailed him, his body shaking with sobs of remorse. But even in the midst of his grief for what might have been, joy spread through him. The joy was for Steven, his son!

The sense of possessive pride he had felt at that moment returned full force, but he knew if he gave in to his desire to hold his son in his arms, he would frighten the child, who was still regarding him with nervous fascination.

To give himself time to regain his self-control, Josh turned his attention back to Diana, his mind again making comparisons. It was true Joanna had been taller than the woman standing in front of him, but still the similarity was striking. Diana was slender as a reed, but by no means skinny, as her rounded breasts testified. He felt a dryness in his mouth as he led them into the living room and was irritated more than ever by the physical impact his sister-in-law was having on him.

As Diana seated herself on the edge of the couch, still clutching Steven to her side, Joshua frowned. Her hair gleamed in the lamp's glow, brown with the fiery highlights he remembered so well, her eyes deep amber pools of promise as she raised her head to look at him. Dear God, he thought. Those glorious, haunting eyes!

Turning his head with an abrupt movement, he knelt down and began talking in a gentle monotone to his son, his heart turning over when he received a shy, dimpled smile for his efforts. Diana didn't protest when he drew the boy away, but he sensed her displeasure and sent her a warning glance from beneath brows only slightly darker than his hair.

Josh had quite sensibly prepared for Steven's visit, and as the child joyfully unwrapped several gaily deco-rated packages containing toys, Diana watched in tense silence. He certainly knows the way to worm himself into a little boy's affections, she thought waspishly. She shifted her position on the couch, trying not to show her irritation at being left so completely to her own devices.

"Steven, Diana's uncomfortable being left all alone," a deep voice mocked. "Why don't you play with your trucks while I go keep her company, hmm?"

The lateness of the hour, which was well past his normal bedtime, and the unaccustomed excitement showed in the truculence of Steven's voice as he cried, "Mama don't care!"

As soon as Steven uttered the appellation, Josh's head moved slowly upward, and he stared in Diana's direction with a darkened flush rising on his cheekbones. That he was furious at Steven's innocent reference to her as his mother was more than evident. He rose to his feet with the taut grace of a cougar, his measured approach seeming just as deadly to the woman he silently stalked.

"Mama?" he questioned, his voice little more than a raspy whisper, but with an underlying violence that caused Diana more than a little discomfort.

With a self-confidence and courage she didn't know she had, she inclined her head in an affirmative gesture, her mouth setting with an implacable firmness that matched his as she said calmly, "What did you expect, Josh? I'm the only mother he's ever had."

At that moment, he found himself staring in unwilling fascination at her face. Although his first reaction had been to think her the image of her sister, he realized that the similarity was only a surface one. Joanna's face had never been that rounded and childish-looking, her nose so small and retroussé.

No! he thought. Joanna's face had been longer, the mouth less full and soft-looking, the chin less rounded. And he was sure she had never had that intriguing dimple which nestled in the middle of an endearingly curved chin. There were other differences that suddenly registered on his consciousness. Diana's face showed a strength of character and a compassion that had been sadly missing in his wife, he thought bitterly.

As if the intensity of his inspection made her uncomfortable, Diana glared at Josh, her breath catching in her throat at the momentary humor that etched itself across his features. For endless seconds she stared at him, unable to comprehend the fleeting tenderness that seemed directed at her.

A petulant remark from Steven caught her attention, and with an overwhelming sense of relief she rose to her feet, a coolly polite smile on her face.

"He's tired," she murmured. "It's time he was in bed."

"You're right," Josh murmured, a wicked glint in his eyes. "Shall I carry him upstairs?"

As he spoke the words Josh watched in satisfaction as her eyes widened with horror. But as she paled alarmingly, he frowned, lowering his head until his cool breath feathered her cheeks.

"For God's sake, Diana," he muttered. "Do you think I'm some kind of a monster who'll insist on wrenching the boy away from you without warning? In case you haven't noticed, the weather's worsened. Even if I were inclined to let you risk your own life, I'm damned if I'll allow you to risk Steven's!"

Diana swayed, holding on to her composure with slender threads. She couldn't prevent the angry retort that rose to her lips, her eyes darkening with something akin to hatred.

"You enjoyed that, didn't you?" she questioned, her voice wobbling uncertainly. "Can you wonder if I find the imagery appropriate?"

Without defending himself, Josh turned on his heel and moved quickly toward his son, not trusting himself to remain close to Diana without resorting to violence. Lord! he thought, lifting the boy onto his shoulders and striding in the direction of the hallway. He couldn't remember when he'd been less in control of his emotions!

"Mama?"

At Steven's alarmed cry Diana forced her legs to move in Josh's direction, smiling up at the child in encouragement.

"It's all right, darling," she soothed. "We're going to spend the night here, in this lovely house."

Josh's long-legged stride never altered, and as they reached the landing at the top of the lushly carpeted stairs her breath was coming in little puffs from the speed of their ascent. Josh threw open a door directly in front of the landing, and Diana sagged with relief when she noticed that the room had twin beds.

Only when Josh handed her a new pair of pajamas for Steven did Diana realize the deviousness in his makeup, and she sent him a glance that spoke volumes. He had planned this, and like a fool she had walked into the trap.

The fault was hers, she castigated herself, mechanically busying her hands with the task of undressing Steven. She hadn't wanted to meet Josh on her home ground, afraid of later being haunted by the memory of his presence there. Now she was paying the price for her foolishness, she raged silently, locking the last snap on the pajama jacket in place with more force than was necessary.

Her anger increased when Steven, artlessly proud of his recent accomplishments, insisted that the "nice" man take him to the bathroom. While they were gone, she carefully folded Steven's clothes and placed them on top of the lovely maple dresser that matched the bed. If she didn't know better, she could swear this room had been decorated purposely with a little boy in mind.

There were twin-framed pictures of engaging animals on the wall above the bed, and the spreads flaunted gaily patterned sailboats against a powder-blue sky. "Even the curtains match," she muttered to herself, turning swiftly with a flush darkening her face, as a deeply amused voice spoke from directly behind her.

"Of course. Did you think I couldn't provide the best for my son?"

"Your son!" she snapped, her eyes sparkling dangerously. "How marvelously well you've suddenly donned the cloak of fatherhood!"

"Not now, Diana," Josh rasped. "Steven's brushing his teeth with rather messy abandon, but he could return at any time. I won't have him upset by all of this, so just keep your voice down."

If it was possible for cheeks to actually burn with fiery intensity, Diana's did in that instant. Fighting back humiliated tears, she was never more relieved than when Steven chose that moment to return. His pride in having brushed his teeth by himself, the amusing contortions of his face as he attempted to show her what a good job he had done, served to lighten the moment with laughter.

She tucked the covers securely around Steven's relaxed little form and bent to kiss him with unself-conscious grace. Sitting on the edge of the bed, she told him a brief version of his big-boy story, immensely relieved when Josh chose that moment to leave the room. By the time she was finished with the tale and moved to tiptoe from the room, Steven was nearly asleep.

The light from the hall would have to serve as a night-light, she decided, opening the door to its widest extent as she switched off the light. As she backed out of the room and came up against a hard, unyielding form, she turned with her heart pounding.

Her eyes were focused on the region of his chest, uncomfortably mesmerized by the soft-looking tufts of golden hair protruding from the open neck of his cream silk shirt. Raising startled eyes, she caught her breath at the expression on his face. She knew, with a sudden sense of shame, that her own scrutiny reflected the same physical awareness leaping between them.

These were the feelings that were an unwanted legacy from the past. She had hated herself for the attraction she felt for her own sister's husband, and she despised herself more now. How could her body trick her into even a momentary weakening of her defenses where this man was concerned? she silently agonized.

Over the years she had deliberately emptied her mind of the power Joshua Cambridge had had over her senses. She hadn't wanted to remember her breathlessness whenever he entered the room or the hollowness she felt in the pit of her stomach whenever he spoke to her in his deep, unconsciously sexy tones. In ignorance of his true character she had practically worshiped the man! But no longer, she determined, taking a deep breath as she stepped past him into the hall.

"Don't wake him," she whispered, subconsciously wanting to halt his progress toward Steven.

With a measured glance he ignored her words, moving toward the bed silently.

A lump formed in her throat as Josh carefully lowered his head until his lips caressed the tousled curls on the pillow. The look on his face held such a wealth of love that she raised the back of her hand to her lips to prevent herself from crying out.

"My little son."

She heard his whisper through a haze of pain, not wanting to accept what her eyes were telling her. No! He didn't have it in him to love. He didn't!

Fighting back her tears, she fled down the stairs, running until she reached the relative impersonality of the living room.

On shaking legs she paced the floor, biting her lips in agitation. What a fool she'd been to come here, she berated herself. She realized that the compulsive attraction she had felt for Joshua Cambridge five years ago hadn't lessened with time, and she wanted to scream out a protest.

She shouldn't feel drawn to the man who had caused Joanna such misery! Did she need her head examined?

she wondered. How could she despise someone and yet hunger for him. With shocked awareness, she realized that her only defense against her emotions must come from forcing herself to remember the things Joanna had told her of her husband's cruelty.

Going to the window, she rested her heated forehead against the coolness of the glass. As she closed her eyes an image of Steven rose up before her, and she nearly moaned aloud in fear . . . the fear of losing him! The look on Josh's face as he had bent over the child returned to haunt her, and she knew without doubt that she had seen a reflection of her own love for her baby in his eyes.

"Don't you think you owe me an explanation?"

Diana hadn't been aware of his return, and with a cry of alarm she turned, hugging her arms defensively around her body.

"Answer me, damn you!"

"There's no need to swear, Josh," she mocked, noting with a welcome air of detachment the muscle pulsing in his clenched jaw. "Although I doubt if you'll like what I'm going to say."

As he stood scowling at her Diana glared right back at him, tilting her head in an unconscious gesture of pride.

"What right do you have to look at me like that?" she remarked cuttingly.

"The right of a father who has been denied all knowledge of his son for over two years."

"A father! You didn't deserve to be a father," she retorted. "From what Joanna told me, you were never even much of a husband."

Josh slid a hand through his hair and turned, sitting down heavily in the canvas chair next to the cavernous rock fireplace that lined the whole of one wall.

She stifled a momentary pang of pity at the sight of the bleak look in his eyes. With a nonchalance she was far from feeling, she sat down on the raised settee built of the same rock adorning the fireplace.

A sense of fatality swept over her as her gaze met the glittering blueness of his eyes from across the small space between them. Involuntarily she shuddered, blaming the shivers coursing through her on the cold seeping through the wall behind her and not on the man staring at her so . . . so strangely.

She moved in nervous reaction when his voice filled the room, the tones harsh and grating.

"Why don't you just get on with it?"

"I . . . I don't know what you want m-me to tell you," she stammered. She was amazed and chagrined that this man, whom she thoroughly despised, seemed to be able to turn her into a stuttering mass of childish confusion and all without any apparent effort. Taking a deep breath to try to steady the quiver in her voice, she asked, "Are you referring to my feelings about you?"

"I want you to explain how you know so much about my marriage to Joanna. I would think all of the . . . intimate . . . details wouldn't have been of much interest to you."

"Joanna might have been five years older, but she was much younger than I in a lot of respects. As her sister, it was my duty to be concerned over the mess she had made of her life."

"Do go on," he drawled, leaning forward and focusing his attention unswervingly on her flushed features.

"When she met and married you while on that modeling assignment in Chicago, the miles separating us didn't prevent our exchanging letters, as you well know. I suspected something was terribly wrong with her marriage to you from the things she wrote, but I didn't guess how horrible an existence she was being forced to lead. Once I learned how burdened she was, I could understand why, when I wrote to tell her of our parents' death in a car crash, I never received a reply."

Josh watched the emotions cross Diana's face as she spoke. She was staring into space, her memories taking her far away from her present surroundings to another time, another place. When she mentioned her parents' death, she was unaware of the look of agony that crossed her features. Silently he cursed Joanna for her callousness in making her sister face such an ordeal alone.

If Joanna had bothered to tell him about the accident, he would have insisted that they return to Los Angeles! he thought savagely. Although the people he remembered hadn't deserved their younger daughter's devotion, he knew that Diana had loved her mother and father, and he was perceptive enough to realize that she still found it difficult to talk about those dark days.

"Anyway," she continued. "I didn't hear from her for a long time after that, nearly a year, in fact. Then one day she turned up at my apartment. She was in a pretty sorry state, six months pregnant, and nearly destitute."

As she uttered these words she slanted him a hostile

look, all the hate for the cause of her lovely sister's misery reflected in her face. "She told me that when she became pregnant you kicked her out. She said you hadn't wanted children and that you blamed her entirely for the condition she was in."

Her words trailed off as she heard his muffled expletive, and she raised startled eyes to his face.

"Well, I took her in and cared for her. It wasn't easy, but that was no fault of hers. I worked as a nursery-school teacher, and although I made a fairly decent salary for one, it was difficult making it stretch for both of us. Then there were the doctor bills, and the thought of what the hospitalization was going to cost nearly made me frantic."

"Why didn't Joanna contact me for support?"

"She told me there wasn't much use, since you would make up some lie about a lover and refuse to support either her or the child, and I had no reason to disbelieve her," she replied, her attitude wholly defensive.

"Didn't it ever enter your head she might be lying?"

"She was all the family I had left," she cried, her face twisted in remembered grief. "There wasn't all that much time to find out the truth. I was too busy just trying to live. Then, when Steven was born, there was no longer any point."

"What the hell do you mean, no point?" he asked, the effort it was costing him to keep his voice moderated showing in his face. "Surely it made even more sense then to contact Steven's only surviving parent!"

"Before Joanna died, she made me promise never to tell you about Steven!"

"My God!" The cry was torn from him, and he jumped to his feet. Abruptly he moved toward the bar and mixed himself a drink with shaking hands.

Looking at him, Diana felt utterly drained. With a despairing moan she leaned forward, supporting her weary head in her hands.

"Here, drink this," Josh demanded, walking toward her with a tall, frosted glass in his grasp.

"Thank you, but I don't want . . ." she began, the words dying on her lips as she met his troubled glance.

"It's just a mild version of a Tom Collins. You look like you can use it."

Even as she took the glass from him she resented the impersonal consideration he was showing for her feelings. She didn't want kindness from this man. She wanted nothing from him, except Steven. He was Steven's father, and although it galled her, she was now in the position of having to stay on the right side of him.

God help her, she thought, if she ever allowed him to see how weak his closeness made her feel. With bewilderment she recognized emotions she had no business feeling, and she lowered her eyes to hide her shameful secret from his discerning gaze.

3

The tense silence lengthened until every nerve in Diana's body was screaming. She could almost feel his eyes boring into her skull, trying to penetrate the closely guarded secrets even she wasn't willing to face.

With a vague feeling of surprise she remembered the glass in her hand and quickly took a large swallow from it, hoping the alcohol would ease some of her tension, help her overcome a regrettable tendency toward tears.

She tried to show no reaction when Josh finally broke the silence, even though the frustration in his voice was obvious. If she didn't respond to the great man's charm in a way to which he was accustomed, that was just too bad, she thought pettily.

"Look, Diana," he muttered. "We're both overwrought and in no condition to make rational judgments at the moment. You think me a selfish, callous brute. Well, I can do without your good opinion. I don't intend to defend my actions either past or present. Not to you or anyone else."

"I'm not asking you to," she retorted, looking at him scornfully. "I don't give a damn!"

"Good. I'm pleased we understand each other." Finishing the last of his drink, he placed the empty glass on the bar.

Imitating his action, she smiled with frosty aloofness. "Thank you for the drink."

"You're welcome!" He didn't return her smile, his eyes seeking to pierce the barrier she was trying to maintain between them. Eventually his mouth curved in a sarcastic smirk, and Diana could feel her resolutions to be coolly polite weakening. Clenching her fists, she resisted the urge to get up and slap that supercilious expression from his face.

Trying to calm herself, she stared down at her hands, forcing her fingers to relax against the material of her powder-blue jumper. She absently studied the cuffed end of her tailored blouse, observing the delicate bones in her wrist with an intensity that surprised her. Anything, she thought, to keep her attention diverted from the man standing much too close for comfort.

Diana heard a muffled expletive, and with a start tried to marshal her wandering thoughts. Their eyes met, and she saw the frustrated impatience of his expression through a veil of nervous anticipation. She had been deliberately shutting him out, and it was quite evident from his reaction that he was fully aware of that fact.

She attempted to apologize for her rudeness, her eyes widening in alarm as his hand viciously sliced the air. He wasn't trying to control his irritation, she realized, almost smiling in amusement at the thought.

"If you say you're sorry when you sure as hell don't mean it," he whispered softly, his glittering gaze holding hers, "I swear I'll strangle you!"

"All right, I'm not sorry," she retorted childishly. "You seem to want everything cut and dried, presented to you with mechanical precision, don't you? Well, I at least am a human being, and as such can't program my emotions as you seem to expect!"

"You're implying that I can?"

"Oh, you can, all right!" She lost all discretion as she met the derisive amusement in his gaze. "You know, Josh. I've hated you for so long now that it's getting to be second nature. The only reason I'm here now is because you've forced my hand, and because I want to make very sure you understand my position. Steven is my only concern, and I won't have him hurt!"

The grooved lines beside his mouth tightened ominously. "Let's get one thing clear, Diana. I didn't travel all this way to hurt my own son. I want to get to know the boy, and considering that I've been a stranger to him until now, that isn't going to be easy. But I will do it! Don't be in any doubt about that. I'm afraid, like it or not, I'll have to insist on your cooperation."

"I don't see why I have to put up with you," she retorted, tilting her head dismissively. "You'll want to have Steven to yourself, no matter how I protest."

"Don't give me that! You couldn't be that naive." He ran his hand over his hair in exasperation. "I'm not the robot you think I am. It would take a blind man not to notice the way the child clings to you." He paused.

"Maybe it would be better to make a clean break. Is that what you want?"

"W-we can arrange suitable visiting times."

A fleeting expression crossed his features, and Diana swallowed past the sudden constriction in her throat. "You're . . . you're not going to take him f-from me?" she whispered, flinching from the harshness of his features. "For God's sake," she cried, feeling sick from the abrupt pounding of her heart. "Think what that would do to Steven!"

Josh remained silent, his eyes studying her with hooded intensity. Her face whitened in shock, fear a coiled knot in her stomach.

"You wouldn't be that cruel." Her eyes filled abjectly. "I've raised him from a baby. You can't expect me to just walk out of his life . . . not entirely."

"Can't I?"

"No, you can't!" Diana could feel her whole body shaking with the force of her feelings. "I've been the one who walked the floor with him when he was cutting teeth. I bathed his body when he was burning with fever. Do you expect me to forget those things, to wipe out the years of loving him?"

"Why not?" He was a suddenly menacing figure as his fists clenched at his sides. "Wasn't it you who denied me those moments in the life of my son?"

She was going to be sick! The thought revolved around and around in her brain. Seeing the accusation on Josh's face convinced her he meant what he said, and with a cry of anguish, she covered her face with her hands.

"For God's sake!" He turned, his hand attempting to

massage away the knotted cord in his neck. "What the hell do you want from me?"

"Please, let him remain with me. If Joanna had lived, and you and she had gotten divorced, you would have had reasonable rights of visitation. W-wouldn't you be willing to work out something along those lines, for Steven's sake as well as both of ours?"

"If Joanna had lived, I'd have had custody of my son," he grated. "She wouldn't have wanted to be burdened with a child for long!"

"That's not true," she gasped. "Joanna would have loved him as much as I do."

Against her will Diana remembered her recent conversation with Elaine. She tried to dismiss the disloyal thoughts, not wanting to be reminded of her sister's bitter attitude toward her pregnancy. Joanna hadn't been herself, she defended the dead woman silently. Her attitude would have changed if only she'd had the chance to see the baby, to hold him in her arms. A pain twisted inside her head, and she flinched from the mocking voice trying to make itself heard.

"Look, neither of us is in the right frame of mind for decisions." Josh sighed, shaking his head defeatedly. "I'm bloody tired, and from the looks of you, you're not feeling much better."

As he spoke he began turning out the lights, continuing to rub the aching muscles in his neck as he moved around the room. Diana stared at him openmouthed, unable to believe he could just walk off in the middle of their conversation. The arrogance of the man, she thought, resentment overriding her common sense.

"I'm going to get Steven," she exclaimed, as he

motioned her to precede him up the stairs. "It's obvious you can't stand the sight of me, and I refuse to stay where I'm not wanted."

"In case you haven't noticed, it's still snowing outside. I have no intention of spending what's left of the night trying to dig my car out of the car port. Even if I were so inclined, I wouldn't let you take Steven from his warm bed in this weather."

"It's a pity you didn't think of that before," she said. "You could have canceled this inquisition the moment we arrived, but nothing would dare interrupt your plans, even the weather!"

"Maybe I did!" His voice was merely a whisper, but it was his eyes that caused her pulse to leap with something verging on panic. Slowly and thoroughly they roamed over her stiffening figure, apparently missing nothing along the way.

The tension between them was almost tangible. When his eyes finally returned to her face, to her dismay she found herself unable to look away. There was something in his expression that went beyond a man-woman awareness, but before she had a chance to grasp its meaning, he turned and headed in the direction of the stairs.

With leaden steps she followed him, all fight going out of her. Drawing a shaky breath, she stood beside the door that he held open for her.

"I think you'll find this room comfortable enough. Good night, Diana."

She watched as without another word he entered his bedroom across the hall, flinching as he shut the door with violence.

Even after a soothing shower, Josh still felt tense. His thoughts were a jumble of unanswerable questions as he dried his body, until his head ached with frustrating indecision.

This was a hell of a situation, he mused, slipping into a white and blue toweling robe and reaching automatically for a cigarette. It took him a moment before he remembered he had quit. With a self-mocking grin he stopped his pacing, turning instead to look for his pipe. Remembering last seeing it in his den, he snorted in exasperation, walking toward the door.

Passing Steven's room, he paused, his mouth curving in a gentle smile. Suddenly he longed for another glimpse of the small boy who was beginning to figure so largely in his life. The door, which had been open when he passed earlier, was now closed. Diana must already have checked on him, he thought, as his hand circled the knob.

The sight that met his eyes stopped him in his tracks, and his breath became suspended in a throat instantly dry. The three-way lamp was turned to its lowest level of illumination, filling the room with a softly sensuous glow. His body leaped into pulsing life as he stared across the room, his eyes drinking in the sight of the woman who hadn't been out of his mind since the moment he had met her again.

She was bending over Steven's bed, her slim fingers tenderly tucking the covers around the sleeping child. His eyes followed the fluid lines of her naked back, moving with masculine appreciation down to where miniscule bikini panties tautened over firmly curved flesh. His breath was a rasping irritation, his attention caught by the shadowy crevice visible through the nearly transparent material.

When Diana turned to slip into the bed beside Steven's, Josh forgot to breathe entirely. A tightening band across his chest was accompanied by a hot flush of arousal, the hardening flesh in his groin aching for a release he couldn't give it.

Her hair was a burnished fire tumbling over creamy shoulders, her breasts high and firm. Completely unaware of his presence, she stretched, muffling a yawn with the back of her hand. Her eyes had closed, but quickly snapped open when she felt the draft from the doorway.

Josh stood there, his eyes glazed with desire as they met hers. For infinitesimal seconds she remained frozen in shock, her muffled gasp echoing his. At the betraying sound uttered low in his throat, she moved to cover herself, a flush spreading over her body. Her arms brushed against the nipples of her breasts, and her flush deepened when she realized they were raised in unwilling arousal.

Her mind registered his silent departure through a haze of self-recrimination. On wooden legs she walked to the door, closed it firmly, and leaned a moist forehead against the coolness of the wood. All she was conscious of was the knowledge that, no matter how much she hated herself, she had enjoyed the feelings generated by Josh's eyes on her body.

The early-morning sun descended like a lance through the tall green pines and speared through Diana's closed eyelids, rousing her from a fitful slumber.

With a groan she rolled over onto her stomach, twisting herself even more tightly into the sheet that gripped her waist.

For a moment she felt disoriented, then with a smothered exclamation she sat up, as full memory returned. She glanced at the bed Steven had slept in the night before and registered the fact that he was no longer in it.

Jumping to her feet, she pulled on her clothes, then she ran her brush swiftly through her tangled hair, not much caring about her appearance. She hurried into the bathroom down the hall, washed her face and cleaned her teeth as well as she was able without a brush. She didn't think Steven could get into much mischief, but she was anxious to get downstairs and make sure.

She was just descending the first step when she paused, hearing muffled laughter coming from the open door of Josh's bedroom. As a deeper, more masculine chuckle followed, a sudden sense of isolation gripped her, and with her lips set mutinously she walked toward the sounds.

"Steven, I . . ." Her voice faltered, a look of consternation crossing her features.

Laughing, Josh looked up and met her widening gaze. She could feel the blush that seemed to be burning her whole body as it had last night. A mocking glint appeared in Josh's eyes as he stretched his lean, muscular body with unself-conscious grace.

With amused comprehension, Josh looked down at his still-giggling son. As she stood, unable to move, he reached down and pulled the sheet up over his naked limbs. Once again he raised his eyes to her face, his knowing smile breaking the frozen stillness that held her. With a muttered apology, she turned and ran from the room, his laughter following her down the stairs.

The sound of that laughter was still ringing in her ears as she entered the kitchen. Placing cold hands against her warm cheeks, she sat down abruptly. Controlling her rapid breathing seemed to be impossible. Every time she thought she had succeeded, she again saw Josh's naked body, his teak-brown skin blatantly sensual against the whiteness of the tangled sheets.

She felt furious with herself, the blood pounding hotly in her veins as if to emphasize the reason for her increased breathing rate. In that instant, when her eyes had surveyed the disturbingly muscular contours of Joshua Cambridge, she had known that he was as aware of her arousal as she was.

She hadn't had the time to hide her reaction, as a tide of blazing heat had raced through her bloodstream . . . the heat of an overpowering attraction. With a despairing groan she visualized his face as it had looked the night before, aware that only moments before her own face had been dark with the same flush of desire.

Jumping to her feet, she nearly ran to the stove. She needed something to take her mind off the image scorching her brain. She turned on the burner of the electric range and searched under the cupboards for a frying pan. When she found one, she set it down with a force that surprised her, then walked to the refrigerator on wobbly legs.

As the omelet slowly simmered in the pan she turned to greet Steven, who burst exuberantly into the room.

"Daddy and me played, Mama."

So it begins, she thought dully. Smiling, she lifted him into a chair, smoothing his rumpled hair with a shaking hand.

"I know you did, sweetheart."

She nearly choked on her reply, but obviously it was enough to satisfy a preoccupied little boy. Washing his face and hands in preparation for the meal was a welcome relief. At least his ceaseless chatter and exuberant presence satisfactorily changed the earlier tenor of her thoughts.

"Good morning!"

The deep rumbling bass of Josh's greeting caused Steven to glance up with a milk ring coating his smiling mouth. Diana felt a strange constriction in her chest at the sight of that trusting smile, as Josh's large hand further rumpled Steven's hair.

She turned, busying herself at the stove. She tipped the large, fluffy omelet out of the pan onto a warmed plate and carried it to the table with jerky footsteps.

"Trying to bribe me?" HIs question was accompanied by a wicked glint in his eyes.

"I wouldn't bother," she retorted, feeling embarrassed as his eyes wandered suggestively over her body. She had pulled her hair back with a rubber band, feeling the need for the severity of the hairstyle. She needn't have wasted her time.

As Josh's eyes searched her face and again lowered to her body, all hope that she could treat him with cold detachment died. She couldn't make herself move away, even though his glance seemed to burn through her clothes where they clung to the fullness of her breasts.

She was caught by the magnetic sensuality of the man seated in front of her. To be honest, she thought in near hysteria, he seemed as fascinated with her as she was with him. She shivered, imagining that his hands were doing the caressing, instead of his eyes.

Seeing the tremor that shook her body, Josh looked up, his own face somber. Steven's chatter melted into the background as they studied each other, and Diana fought the urge to cross her arms defensively over her breasts. She knew his eyes hadn't missed the fact that she wasn't wearing a bra. Even now she could feel the involuntary hardening of her nipples from his raking inspection.

She almost sobbed with relief when Steven tipped over his milk. The resulting confusion broke the spell holding her. With feverish haste she mopped at the spill.

"Aren't you going to eat?" Josh's voice fell just short of being demanding. Rinsing out the washcloth, she kept her back to him as she replied.

"I'm not very hungry."

"Sulking, Diana?"

"I'm not sulking, Josh, much as it must annoy you to hear it," she returned, using anger as a shield against her vulnerability. She felt an urge to run from the antagonism between them, but instead said, "I wonder how long it'll be before the roads are clear?"

"So anxious to leave?" he mocked. "Weren't the accommodations comfortable, Diana?"

"Stop it, Josh!"

She turned in time to see his quick frown, his narrow-eyed gaze impaling her.

"I only thought you and Steven might like to spend the weekend here," he remarked.

"Thank you, but I have a lot to do at home."

"That's that, then," he said, getting to his feet. "As soon as the roads are passable I'll drive you home. I'll see that your car is returned," he insisted, halting her protest with a negligent wave of his hand. "It won't take you long to pack an overnight case for Steven, will it?"

Before she could protest, Josh turned to the child. "Would you like to spend the weekend here, son?"

His face alight with excitement, Steven began bouncing in his chair. "Can I, Mama? Can I?"

Realizing she no longer had any choice in the matter, if she ever had, she forced a smile. Nodding agreement, she turned away before the little boy noticed the tears forming in her eyes.

"Don't, Diana!"

With a strangled moan, she turned toward the sound of the strangely tormented voice. She hadn't heard his approach. He must walk as silently as a cat, she thought nervously, her eyes widening at the grimness of his expression.

"Don't what?" Her voice was barely audible, her heart pounding at his closeness.

"Don't . . . this," he replied, brushing her cheek gently.

Wanting to close her eyes at the intensity of her response, she fought back instead in the only way she could.

"What do you expect, when you deliberately use Steven's excitement over acquiring a father against me?"

"I wasn't trying to do anything of the kind, and you know it! He's my son, and I want the chance to build a relationship. Is that so difficult to understand?"

"Don't lie!" She was disgusted when the flow of tears refused to be stemmed. "You want to punish me for not letting you know about him. Don't you have even the smallest scrap of human warmth? I know you plan to take him away from me; you've made that more than clear. And I'm dying inside!"

She was unaware of anything but her fear and grief. She was drowning, and only Josh could save her. With a feeling of horror she realized she couldn't blame him if he hated her. She had cost him more than two years of his son's life, and that in itself was unforgivable.

She was so busy castigating herself that she almost didn't hear his next words. After he had stalked angrily from the room, they seemed to hang in the air around her, piercing her heart with a fierce hope.

"For heaven's sake, quit sniveling. If there's one thing I can't fight, it's the love of a mother for her child!"

The love of a mother . . . Getting Steven bathed and dressed, she couldn't stop herself from contemplating the significance of Josh's words.

Had it been her imagination, or had he actually acknowledged her own claim to his son? She was almost afraid to believe that the love she felt for the child would alter Josh's determination to get custody. What if she were wrong, and this was only his way of extending her torment? Would he dangle Steven like a prize in front of her, relax her defenses, and then snatch him away?

After taking Steven downstairs, she watched with burning eyes as he joined Josh outside. She could see his hands waving, the smile-dimpling cheeks flushed from the cold. She saw Josh motion Steven toward the path curving along the lake, his hand gently lying on the small head as they stood together beneath the pines.

She felt oddly neglected, shut off from the tableau of a father with his son. Her teeth clenched together when Josh turned, reached down, and lifted the boy into his arms. Steven's chubby arms circled a strong neck, and his head bent to place a kiss on the face so near to his own.

She groaned as she saw Josh's face convulse with emotion, his arms clasping the child as if he would never let him go. For the first time Diana realized the enormity of the wrong she had done Joshua Cambridge. She had played God by giving in to Joanna's demand that Josh be denied his own son, and now she would pay.

She tried to justify her actions by remembering what Josh had done to her sister, but she was no longer able to dredge up her earlier hatred. In an unbelievably short space of time he had convinced her of his ability to love Steven.

No matter how much she wanted to deny it, she knew that Joanna had lied to her. The monster her sister described had existed only in her tortured imagination, she was sure of it. No man could change so much in such a short space of time.

Although admitting this to herself increased her remorse, Diana felt strangely contented. A smile curved her lips, and a fleeting tenderness flowed outward toward the two she now watched so avidly. She wasn't aware of them intermingling in her mind, tiny beloved features becoming superimposed on another, more mature countenance.

She couldn't help noticing the similarity of their stance. Already Steven was imitating the man, who must have seemed wonderful to a little boy whose existence had been devoid of masculine example. For the first time, she understood what she would be denying the child she loved if she attempted to cling to the exclusive relationship they had shared in the past. A little boy needs a father, she realized, clenching her hand against the window frame.

She refused to listen to the voice that murmured to her from deep inside herself. She wouldn't acknowledge its presence, even though the message seemed permanently imprinted on her consciousness. Shaking her head in repudiation didn't have the desired effect, and again she heard her inner voice ask, "What about your needs, Diana?"

4

~~~~~~~~~~~~

Her small cottage was warm and welcoming, but Diana found no comfort there. It had been late afternoon before the roads were clear enough for her to return home. Josh followed her car, staying only long enough to collect Steven's clothing. His manner was withdrawn as she handed him the small case, becoming almost hostile when Steven clung to her briefly before following his father out the door.

Good Lord! What in the world did he expect? Pacing the living room floor, she bit her lip and remembered the slight trembling in Steven's body as she hugged him. Until that moment he hadn't realized that she wouldn't be going with them. The fact that Steven went at all said a lot for Josh's ability to charm small boys into blind adoration. Otherwise she was certain Steven would have refused to leave.

She had visions of him waking in the night, crying for her. They had never been apart before. She should be there to tuck him into bed, hear his prayers, and feel his soft little mouth against her cheek.

Wrapping her robe more closely around her, she shivered. The bath she had taken earlier had done nothing to help her relax. At the rate she was going from room to empty room, her feet would be killing her by morning.

With a sigh she moved toward her desk. Sleep would be impossible under the circumstances, so maybe work was the answer. She had to study the applications for employment Elaine had asked her to look over, and now was as good a time as any. They needed to take on more students, and if they did that, they would have to hire another teacher. The law stipulated that preschools must have one adult for a certain number of children, and although they had recently added to their payroll a young woman who needed to supplement the family income, both she and Elaine agreed that their next employee should have college credentials. That way they would achieve a nice balance, and the parents could be assured of the very best of care for their youngsters.

A muffled thud caused her to swivel in the direction of the door. She had been fully engrossed, managing to block her earlier disturbing thoughts from her mind. When another thud sounded, she felt her mouth go dry. What in the world? she wondered.

"Diana, let us in!"

With a worried frown she pulled the chair free, her fingers fumbling with the lock. Finally managing to get the door open, she stared at the blanketed figure in Josh's arms and reached out involuntarily, only to be halted by their abrupt entry.

Closing the door after them, she turned and followed Josh as he headed in the direction of Steven's room.

"What's the matter? Is he all right?"

Josh ignored her anxiously whispered questions, silently and efficiently divested Steven of both blanket and robe, and tucked him into bed.

Bending down after Josh left the room, she noticed tear-stained cheeks, and swiftly drew her own conclusions. Her brief sense of triumph disappeared when she heard a muffled sob and small quivering lips asking, "Mama?"

"I'm here, darling," she whispered, brushing the silky hair from his damp forehead. "You're home with me, so go back to sleep."

The silken lashes flickered once, twice, and were still as the small boy relaxed into a deep sleep. Placing a light kiss on his gently rounded cheek she tiptoed from the room, making sure the night-light was burning before closing the door.

"What happened?"

Josh was standing by the window, staring out into the darkness. At the sound of her voice, he turned.

"He kept screaming about a 'big-boy story,' whatever that is. Why are you looking so upset? Wasn't this what you were counting on?"

"I don't know what you're talking about."

"Don't you, Diana?"

Her control finally gave way, and she shook her head in violent negation. "For heaven's sake," she snapped, crossing her arms defensively around her upper body. "Steven's barely more than a baby. You've got to give him time to get used to being shuttled back and forth between us."

With a jerky movement he ran his hand through his hair, and Diana watched as it again fell forward. She saw the same vulnerability in his face that she had noticed in Steven's only moments before. She moved toward him, placing a consoling hand on his muscled forearm.

"Josh, I'm sorry," she whispered, her eyes widened with emotion as they met his own. "He just needs a little more time."

"Damn it, he needs more than time," he insisted, grasping her shoulders and shaking her. "He needs his mother!"

Diana tensed. No matter what Joanna had done to him in leaving, he obviously still loved her . . . hungered for her. It was there in his voice, a desire so raw she flinched from it. She didn't want to know why that thought hurt so much.

"His mother's dead," she remarked dully, her mouth trembling. "I've done the best I could to make it up to him."

"Look at me, Diana."

His voice was strained. She lifted her head and they studied each other silently. As the moments passed she found herself stifled by a blaze of emotion in eyes so piercing that they seemed to see inward to her very soul.

"His mother's very much alive," he whispered, an almost wondering expression crossing his somber features. "You're the mother of his heart, Diana. You're all I could ask for as a mother for my son, don't you realize that? So gentle and loving . . ."

She wanted to run, to pull herself away from the spell he was weaving around her, but her legs wouldn't function. Her will was being reduced until it was no larger than the image of herself reflected in his eyes, and she had the hysterical idea that if she didn't escape soon, she never would!

"Let me go!" Her frantic whisper went unheeded. His hands, which a few moments before were punishing bands on her flesh, gentled. His thumbs rubbed her tender skin rhythmically, and panic fluttered in her throat as his mouth began to curve sensually.

Almost as if he were unaware of his own words, he began to speak, and Diana knew that never before had she felt the depth of hurt engendered by his soft voice.

"You're as beautiful as she was," he murmured, drawing her inert body against his hard length. "Yet there's a difference, do you know that? Joanna's eyes never reflected the fire in her hair, the way yours do."

His husky voice was a muted rumble in her ear, and with a shock she felt his lips teasing at the lobe, his tongue entering and sending a whirl of sensations flooding through her awakening body.

"Lovely, haunting eyes," he moaned.

"Damn you, I'm not Joanna," she cried, desperate now to escape arms that were attempting to revive a love long dead.

Ignoring her words, he grasped her head firmly. His fingers curled in her hair and levered her face upward. She opened her mouth to protest. Seeing his advantage, he quickly lowered his head to cover her lips with his own.

The kiss was hotly arousing, completely draining what little resistance she had left, and she sagged in his arms. As she relaxed against him he groaned low in his throat, his kiss wilder as he parted her mouth further to allow a full exploration of its sweet moistness.

Josh felt his body hardening and pressed himself against the softness of her trembling thighs. God! he thought, in an agony of wanting. The taste of her, the smell, the feel of her body was good, so damn good!

He couldn't remember ever feeling like this. Somehow Diana had gotten under his guard, which hadn't been let down in years. He was having trouble remembering who she was, or why this was happening. And, he admitted to himself honestly, at the moment he couldn't care less. He would probably hate himself in the morning, but tonight he was turned on as he had not been in a long, long time. It was sweet, so very sweet. . . .

His sensual thoughts were interrupted when at last he extended the kiss to the enticing hollow of the base of her smooth throat and felt the sob that wrenched her body. Lifting his head, he noticed the tears trickling slowly from closed eyelids.

"Is my touch so distasteful, little one?"

As he asked the question he ran a gentle finger across her softly flushed cheek. As if the very tenderness of his touch gave her courage that she had been lacking only moments before, Diana forced her eyes open.

"I don't understand you." She sighed, shaking her head. "Is this your way of punishing me?"

His body stiffened, and the coldness she hated reappeared in his eyes. "What the hell do you mean?"

"I . . . I took Steven, and . . . and didn't let you know about him. You hate me, don't you?"

As though he couldn't bear the sight of her, he released her so suddenly she almost cried out. I don't understand myself, she thought.

She didn't want to be used to alleviate his longing for Joanna, and yet she needed every shred of strength she possessed to prevent herself from pressing against the rigid back now turned in her direction. Only seconds before she had wanted to escape from his arms, and now that she had, she felt cold and almost . . . bereft.

Grasping the back of a chair for support, she watched with glazed eyes as he moved toward the door. The air blew into the room in an icy blast, and she clenched her teeth to keep them from chattering. She was beyond speaking, beyond feeling anything but dull, aching misery.

"Don't you think I have reason to hate you, Diana?"

The question took her by surprise. Her face whitened as she stared at him. At that moment she would have given nearly everything she possessed not to have to answer, but found herself nodding in agreement.

He closed the door, keeping his hand on the knob. "The proper authorities didn't try to locate Steven's father because you told them that I was dead and you were the boy's only living relative."

"You know?" The words were nothing more than a pitiful gasp.

"From the beginning," he admitted.

"But why didn't you say anything?"

"Because I'm not the unfeeling bastard of Joanna's imagination," he muttered, rubbing the back of his neck tiredly. "I understand your motives, all of them. You wanted to protect Steven from the man Joanna accused me of being, and at the same time didn't want to lose him yourself. The situation we now find ourselves in is of your making, but not entirely. If I had been the kind of husband Joanna needed, I wouldn't have missed out on a large part of my son's life. In our own way we've both failed Steven, and it's got to stop. There'll be no more talk of hating between us—for his sake. Agreed?"

"Yes, Josh."

The change in his expression was instantaneous, and she found herself staring at the smile curving his mouth. He turned to leave, and she moved urgently toward the door.

"Josh?"

He stopped, his eyes lingering on her face while one brow tilted upward in inquiry.

"You didn't know Joanna was pregnant when she left, did you?" she whispered.

"I didn't know," he affirmed, his eyes never leaving hers.

"I'm . . . I'm so sorry for what I've done to you," she admitted, lowering her gaze to the tip of her cream satin slippers. "I knew Joanna wasn't well. I shouldn't have been so ready to believe . . ."

She almost gasped as his large hand cupped her chin, raising her head until she was forced to meet his eyes.

"Shall we try for a new beginning?"

She nodded, her own mouth curving gently. "Please!"

During the following months Diana's relationship with Josh developed into a wary neutrality. Josh, planning various amusements which appealed to a small boy, centered much of his attention on Steven.

One outing stood out in her memory. Spring had come, bringing a fragrant surge of new life. The air was warm, melting the patches of snow remaining on the ground, and tiny flowers and grasses blossomed forth from the rich earth.

They left town and headed toward Emerald Bay State Park. When they reached the park, they took a footpath that led down to the shore of the lake, where Vikingsholm, an authentic reproduction of a Viking castle, stood.

While they sauntered back up the path toward Josh's car, he carried a tired Steven. They talked quietly over the head of the small boy, and Diana felt at peace, treasuring the transitory closeness with the man at her side.

"You're very good with children," she found herself saying. They had reached the top of the path, the beautiful panorama of Emerald Bay spread out around them.

"I like kids." His voice, though subdued, sounded harsh with bitter memory as he glanced at the russet head nestled inside the curve of his arm.

Before she had time to think, or to even realize what she was going to say, she blurted, "I know. Don't torture yourself!"

Josh smiled at her with a natural sincerity that caught at her heart. She had never before voiced her belief in him, and she was rewarded by the tenderness in his eyes. With surprise she realized how hungry she had become for such a look!

To relieve the tension, she asked, "How do you research your books, Josh?"

As soon as the question was out of her mouth she flushed, averting her head to escape the amusement in his eyes. He obviously hadn't missed her rather inane attempt to avoid a more personal conversation, but to her relief he responded without mentioning it.

"Much of the research can be done in libraries, but I like to personally get the feel of the settings of my books by following the paths my characters walk, and by talking with the people who live in those areas."

"Do people hold back?" she asked, her brow tilting inquiringly as she slanted a glance in his direction. "You'd be a stranger, after all."

Josh's laughter was rich and full, and Diana felt a flicker of pleasure against her spine. Absently skirting the exposed root of an evergreen after stumbling like an idiot, her embarrassment grew when she realized she hadn't heard his answer.

"Do you, Diana?"

"I'm sorry," she mumbled, looping her hair behind her ear. "I'm afraid I didn't hear a word you were saying. I must be getting deaf in my old age."

"If you're an example of the elderly, then I hope I live to be Methuselah," he teased, obviously enjoying the deepening color in her cheeks. To her relief he decided it was time to take pity on her and end her obviously uncomfortable confusion. He told her how much he enjoyed making friends when he traveled and how much of themselves people gave when they came to understand the sincerity of his interest.

"Do you enjoy people, Diana?"

Her hesitation was brief. "I've loved some of the individuals who have touched my life at one time or another, but sometimes it's difficult for me to show it. I . . . I'm shy, and find myself wondering what to say to them."

Silently he studied her features, until a slow, warm smile spread across his face. "I know, honey. It's all there in your eyes."

Steven chose that moment to waken, and she found herself relaxing as they finished their walk to the car. With a few quiet words Josh halted the child's protests at returning home, much to Diana's chagrin. If it had been she Steven was arguing with, she knew from experience he wouldn't have given up so easily!

Often she found her thoughts returning to their trip to Emerald Bay. In retrospect, the whole outing had been bathed in golden promise, but as the days passed without a recurrence of the closeness between herself and Josh, she grew increasingly frustrated. Although she was grateful for the chance to understand her own feelings about him, she became irritated by his impersonal attitude. The passion that had flared so briefly between them sometimes seemed a figment of her imagination, until her body quickened with the memory.

Today he was due to pick up Steven, and her loneliness enclosed her like a shroud. She would again throw herself into her work at the school, but somehow the satisfaction she normally derived from her career was lessened since Josh had entered their lives.

"Mama, I'm through."

"So you are, honey." She smiled. "Did you have enough to eat?"

He nodded, tilting his head and studying her with hopeful eyes. "Front yard?"

"All right." She laughed. "But only if you promise not to wander off. Daddy will be here soon."

Eager for the out-of-doors, Steven hopped from foot to foot as she wiped his face free of cereal.

"Steven, if you'll quit wriggling long enough for me to clean you up, you'll be able to go outside a lot sooner," she finally muttered in exasperation. "There. Now, go fetch your jacket, and I'll fasten it for you."

A mulish light entered the eyes raised toward her face. "I'll do it," he demanded. "My daddy says I'm a big boy!"

At Steven's unexpected burst of defiance, Diana's lips firmed into a hard line. It wasn't like him to challenge her like this, and she wasn't quite sure how to handle it. Things had been bound to change, now that he had a father to emulate, but she was bothered by the nature of the changes. She might no longer be the center of his existence, but she wasn't going to stand for disrespect.

"Steven, you'll go get your coat and come back here immediately, do you understand?"

He pouted, his feet dragging as he headed for his

room. Diana sighed with relief, doubting her ability to cope with a tantrum this morning. She began washing the breakfast dishes.

Laying the last bowl on the drying rack, she felt the beginning of a headache punishing her temples. The ring of the doorbell didn't do much to improve her mood, and she ushered Josh inside with ill-mannered abruptness.

"What's the matter?" He laughed. "If you don't take that scowl off your face, I might begin to think I'm annoying you."

Forcing herself to relax, she apologized. "I guess I got up on the wrong side of the bed this morning."

"If you want cheering up, just look out the window. That's an exceptional pile of dirt our boy's building."

With a muffled exclamation she turned, pulling aside the drape with barely controlled anger. The sight of Steven, playing happily after deliberately defying her, seemed to be the last straw. She knew she was overreacting, but she couldn't seem to curb her outburst.

"I won't have it," she stormed, turning furiously and glaring at Josh. "Until you came Steven never thought of open disobedience."

"What's eating you?" he groaned, shaking his head in impatience.

"I told him to bring me his coat so I could help him with it. He wanted to do it himself, and as you can see, that's exactly what he did."

"What do you expect?" He lowered his long frame onto the couch, while his eyes accused her of childishness. "Steven's not the baby you're trying to keep him, Diana. I think he's capable of putting on his own coat."

Biting her lip, she glared at him. "That's not the point. I know it seems petty, but he's never deliberately defied my authority before."

"Meaning?"

At his low, menacing question, she hesitated. It wasn't fair to blame Josh for his son's behavior, she realized. She was as much at fault. Lately, she had been preoccupied, less receptive to Steven's needs. Since Josh kept Steven with him during the day while she worked, he saw much more of the boy than she did. Wasn't it natural for Steven to develop independence, after being forced from his familiar routine?

Unable to endure Josh's inspection, she crossed to the small fireplace now littered with the blackening of last night's fire.

"Just what were you implying just now, Diana?"

"N-nothing, really. I . . ."

"What kind of man would I be to encourage my own son to show disrespect to you or any other woman?"

"That's just it," she cried. "I don't really know what kind of man you are," she replied, her voice strained.

"Then you'd better start making up your mind, or this whole thing isn't going to work worth a damn!"

Closing her eyes in defeat, she leaned her forehead against the mantle. He was right, she thought. Her feelings for Josh were beginning to overcome everything else, frightening her into acting completely out of character. The resentment she directed at him on numerous occasions left him thinking her as disrespectful as Steven, and she couldn't blame him. She didn't want to ask herself why she needed to keep him at arm's length. She knew she wouldn't like the answers.

"You're right, I was overreacting. I don't know what's the matter with me."

"I do."

Stiffening, she turned to him. She wanted to look away, but found she couldn't.

"You're afraid you'll lose Steven to me," he said, his voice quiet. She almost wished he had shouted at her. Then she could have fought the truth of what he was saying. As it was, his modulated tone lent the words strength, forcing her to analyze them.

Her concentration was so deep that she missed Josh's almost silent approach until he stood before her. She uttered a startled cry when his hand cupped her chin and tilted her head back until their eyes met.

"Am I right?"

"I . . . I," she stammered, her pulses throbbing erratically. She tried to move her head away from his touch but was prevented by the increased pressure against her jaw. Moistening instantly dry lips with the tip of her tongue, she tensed as she gave the answer he was waiting for. "You're right. Please, let me go, Josh."

He stiffened. His face became a harshly chiseled mask, his thoughts hidden. She was surprised when he turned abruptly, moving to throw open the door. He shouted for Steven, and almost immediately she was staring into the child's tear-drenched eyes.

"I'm sorry!"

Josh took Steven by the hand, leading him onto the front porch. Kneeling down beside the boy he began talking. She heard snatches of words, and surprisingly enough, a peeling laugh from Steven. At that sound, relief flooded her, and as Josh reentered the room, she met him with a tremulous smile.

Her grin faded as she was faced with a brooding stare.

He closed the door without removing his eyes from hers, and moved toward her slowly.

"Josh, I . . ."

The smile curving his lips never reached his eyes. There was a leashed quality in his actions which made her want to flee, but instead she found herself stupidly waiting for his wrath to fall. That he was angry she had no doubt. All the signs were there, easy enough to read in the pallor of his face, the bleakness of his expression.

"I've tried to give you time to get to know me," he whispered, hard hands reaching out and clasping her shoulders. "But no matter how hard I try, I can't seem to penetrate that wall of prejudice you've placed between us. I've reached the end of my patience, Diana. There's only one way to reach you, and I mean to take it . . . now!"

He began to pull her closer, and she shivered. She couldn't allow him to degrade her by his anger, she couldn't! She cared too much, loved him too much, to let him do this to both of them. Pushing frantically against his chest, she lifted a face filled with remorse.

"Don't you understand?" she whispered, shaking her head in defeat. "How else can I fight the way you make me feel? It's wrong, Josh. You loved Joanna, but she's dead. I won't sacrifice myself, even for you."

The hands that clasped her so tightly loosened and

slid upward over her shoulders until they circled her throat. She was held fast by the depth of emotion leaping between them, her body crying out for the solid comfort his could offer.

"I don't want a sacrifice," he murmured, his tongue gently stroking the corner of her lips. "I'm asking for a gift!"

5

Pale cream walls swirled and dipped as she stared at Josh. His words seemed to hang between them, filling the air with emotion.

"Gifts must be paid for." Her voice was little more than a whisper. "Who's going to settle the bill, Josh?"

"Tell me it wouldn't be worth the price, little one."

He pulled her closer as he spoke, and something seemed to snap inside of her. Without thinking she raised her hand to ward off his descending mouth, horrified when her fingernail scratched the side of his face. She jerked back against his circling arms, unable to glance away from the angry-looking welt.

"I didn't mean to hurt you."

"I'm used to hurting, honey." A slow smile curved his mouth. "You can take the pain away. That's the gift I want from you. Won't you kiss me better, love?"

The negative movement of her head was completely automatic. A part of her ached to respond to the seductive promise in his whispered words, but she didn't dare give in to the longing in his voice. Then there would be no going back, she realized.

She knew he was hurting from the pain of a love long lost, but she couldn't bring herself to feel compassion. She was suffering, too, wanting a love that would never be hers. Oh, Josh! she cried silently. I would be giving you everything, but what would I receive in return?

Josh's hand moved from her back to her neck, and his thumb slid in a gentle caress against her jaw. She couldn't stop the shiver of reaction anymore than she could stop breathing. She began to tremble.

"Oh, God! Don't look at me like that. I wouldn't hurt you. I only want . . ."

Moistening her lips, she drew in a steadying breath. "You only want me, Josh? Do you think you're the only man to say that to me? Doesn't what I want matter to you?"

"You want me!" As he uttered the statement his palm moved to cover the pulse leaping in her throat. "Don't you recognize this awareness for what it is, honey? Let me love you, Diana. I won't ask for more than you're willing to give. Just let me show you how good it can be between us."

She didn't know whether to laugh or cry. It wasn't love he was offering her. Why couldn't he see that? she wondered. Was it possible for him to have convinced himself that the emotions she had revived were for her alone, and not a part of his need to have Joanna back again? He had admitted that he had not been the husband her sister needed, and now he was trying to alleviate the guilt he carried. He wanted to go back, to have another chance, but she couldn't allow herself to be used as a replacement for the woman he still loved!

"No, Josh. In my mind, you'll always belong to Joanna. I'm sorry if that isn't what you want to hear, but I can't help the way I feel."

Josh didn't show, by even the flicker of an eyelash, the pain her words caused him. His hand tightened briefly against the soft underside of her jaw, but his narrowed eyes held the torment of an animal caught in a trap. He couldn't undo the past, he realized. Although he wanted to give her everything he had to give, she didn't want what he offered. She asked for the impossible, and the knowledge caused familiar bitterness, releasing the control he was exercising over his emotions.

In thickened tones he asked, "So you expect me to respect your feelings? What about mine, Diana? Sweet heaven, you're driving me insane!"

The tension vibrating from him excited her, and she stared at the rapid pulse beating in his throat. Her own heartbeat echoed his as he drew her inexorably closer to his hard, muscular frame.

Dear God! she thought. She had never before been so aware of a man's body! She felt as if she were burning where her soft thighs were crushed against their rigid male counterpart and where her tender breasts were pressed against his solid chest.

She felt humiliated by her own lack of control, and a

flush spread over her neck and face. She couldn't help but notice his own awareness of her reaction to him; it was there in the feverish excitement in his eyes and in the trembling of the firm hands that moved to caress her.

"No!" Even as she uttered the cry, she used the gentling of his grasp to get away from him. Taking him by surprise, she turned and ran toward the hallway. When she heard him right behind her, she used her last ounce of speed to try to reach the bathroom, which had the only interior lock in the house.

She wouldn't be able to hide in there forever, but hopefully she would gain the time she needed. She had to come to grips with her desire to give Josh whatever he asked of her. She had nearly reached the sanctuary of the bathroom, her hand within reach of the door-knob, when she felt strong fingers gripping her arm, spinning her around before her instinctive cry of defeat could be uttered.

Almost immediately the pitiful sound was smothered as demanding lips covered her mouth, and her head was forced against the closed door. His arms held hers locked firmly to her sides. As his kiss ravaged her sensitive mouth a moan escaped her and her eyes filled with tears.

"Don't cry," he whispered, a tremor shaking his body when he lifted his mouth from hers. Although she saw remorse darkening his eyes, she knew from the determination tightening his jaw that her pleas would go unheard. He licked the tears from her cheek before he once again found her throbbing mouth.

He coaxed her tenderly, brushing his lips softly against hers. With an inner sob, she felt his body press hers against the unyielding hardness of the door, despair gripping her when a flicker of flame shot through her midsection and spread spears of delight throughout her body. Trying to resist him just fanned the flame of his ardor, as his mouth devoured hers with a strangely gentle ferocity, and his head moved back and forth seductively.

Her trembling legs stopped supporting her and only the pressure of his body kept her from falling. All of her resistance fled, melting into nothingness. He seemed to sense the instant of her capitulation. His arms no longer pinned hers to her sides, and she clutched at his shoulders. She felt the soft velour of his shirt under her hands, and her fingers sensitively roamed the bunched muscles of his chest.

As if to reward her for her compliance, Josh drew her even more fully against him, and his hands ran down her body to her hips in a single caress, which left her shuddering in response. He lifted his head, and stared into her eyes, his breath caught at the passion that transformed them into huge amber pools set against the whiteness of her face.

His eyes remained, trapped and drowning with need, while his hand moved against her hip. Not satisfied to remain inert, his other hand traveled upward over her stomach, sensitive to the muscles knotting against his fingers. The involuntary response intensified his excitement and beads of moisture glistened on his forehead.

"Tell me it's good." He looked to her mouth for a

response, his glance trapped by swollen sweetness. When she remained stubbornly silent, he smiled, and his hand crept underneath her loose sweater.

"Don't touch me . . . Please!" Her exclamation was forced from her with an accompanying shudder, as his hand closed over the fullness of her bare breast.

"Don't you like the feel of my hand, sweetheart?" His voice rumbled against her ear, and she groaned as she felt his moist tongue circling the lobe. "Don't you?" This time the question was accompanied by the movement of his thumb against her nipple, which rose to his touch like a thirsty flower seeking rain.

"No . . . no . . . no!" The lying chant faltered into a low moan, as his hand raised her sweater, and his tongue licked across the throbbing peak. The moment his lips circled the tiny bud in a gentle sucking motion, she was lost. Her hands captured his head, burying themselves in the luxuriant thickness of his hair.

The desire to escape was gone. Now she only wanted to cling to the moment, and she rhythmically arched her body in time to the movements of his mouth. She was aware of an intensity of sensation she hadn't even known existed, and no longer questioned the pleasure that spread from her swollen breasts throughout her body. Another shudder wracked her body as she felt his teeth bite gently into the soft flesh before he once again soothed the darkened aureole with his tongue.

Diana was beyond protest when he quickly and surely lifted her into his arms, and her head fell back against his shoulder as if it belonged there. With determined steps he carried her into her bedroom, slammed the door shut with his foot, and laid her down on the chenille spread.

Momentarily he stared down at her, his breathing fast and uneven. He tore the shirt from his sweat-slickened body, his hands clumsy in their haste. Removing his belt with frustrated impatience, he lowered himself onto the bed, anxious to hold her in his arms.

"Daddy . . . Daddy! I want to come in."

"God, not now!" Josh's groan was accompanied by the movement of his body as he rolled away from her. He threw his arms across his eyes and fought for control.

Diana heard Steven's voice with a feeling of relief. She would have done it! She would have let him take her and she would have reveled in the taking, she thought, shame washing over her.

"Wait here for me, honey," he whispered, bending to brush his lips lingeringly against her throat.

"Please, just go to Steven." She was disgusted by the plea in her voice and refused to meet his eyes.

"Daddy, where are you?" Steven sounded frightened now, and with a muffled curse and a last lingering look at Diana, Josh got up from the bed. His gold gabardine slacks still beltless and slung low on his narrow hips, he walked toward the bedroom's sliding glass door and stepped out onto a small redwood deck.

"I'll be right there, son."

"Okay, Daddy," Steven yelled back, relief in the childish treble.

Reentering the room, Josh's eyes darkened angrily at the sight of Diana straightening her clothes. She met his gaze defiantly. Only the slight trembling of her fingers gave evidence of her continued distress, and he found himself resenting her calm when he was still so aroused. She brushed the hair from her face, her body taut as she rose to her feet.

"I'll go down to him," she mumbled and lowered her eyes from his scowling face.

"That's right, Diana. Run away like a good little girl." As he uttered the words he reached for his shirt. Slipping his arms in the sleeves, he tucked it loosely into his pants.

"Josh, you're not being fair."

"Maybe not, but you don't have to look so damn pleased about it."

She understood his feelings, because she shared them. She ached with unfulfilled longings, her body crying out for the satisfaction it had been denied. Disappointment was making him react with anger. He couldn't get to the relief of tears, as she could. She only wished she could hate him, but she couldn't. When she tried to summon resentment, she found herself remembering the way her skin had hungrily responded to his touch.

Diana heard his footsteps cross the floor. Still trapped inside her own misery, she heard the door open and Steven ask for her. Josh's mumbled reply was indistinct. By the sound of his voice she knew he was leading Steven away from the hallway, thus giving her time to compose herself.

Shaking herself free from her somnolent state, she realized she was still standing beside the rumpled bed. Her bed, she thought. But it had almost become their bed! Biting her lip in consternation, she groaned. Concentrating on placing one foot in front of the other, she stumbled from the room.

Reaching the security of the bathroom, she brushed some order into her tumbled hair and noticed with disgust the kissed look of her mouth. Lifting the sweater away from her tender breasts, she moaned, still able to feel the imprint of his mouth and hands on her flesh.

Distressed by this evidence of his near possession, she jerked the sweater down over her feverishly warm body and ran toward her room. She reached into the closet to withdraw her brown corduroy jacket and put it on with frantic haste. As she slid the zipper all the way up to her neck she turned with determination and walked past the sliding doors into the stand of trees behind the house. She relished the sound of the bracken crunching beneath her heel, because every step spelled freedom for a while.

Steven would be all right with Josh, and she needed to be alone, to try and walk off this nervous tension tearing at her insides. She knew the reason for her restlessness, and the knowledge left a bitter taste in her mouth.

After this morning, their relationship could never be the same, and the thought terrified her. For the first time she admitted to herself that the teeth of the trap had truly and finally closed shut on her. She could never convince Josh she felt nothing for him, when her body had told him just the opposite. She had taken a small bite of the fruit she had always considered forbidden, and she wanted more.

Diana bit her lip, fighting back tears of self-pity. She

would continue to hide her love from him, but after today she could never convince him that she didn't want him. She could no longer hide, from herself or Josh, the dark and inexplicable attraction he held for her. Even the knowledge that he shared the same obsession brought no relief. Her wants were for the man, while his stemmed from a need to recapture the love he had known with Joanna.

She had more reason than most to know that loving didn't always mean being loved in return. She seemed to have spent her whole life doing the loving, while her feelings were met with indifference by the people she tried to draw close. Was she fated to care without ever knowing what it was like to be cared about? she wondered.

Stop it, Diana! Even as she silently issued the command, her true nature began to reassert itself. She was one of the world's givers, and she knew she received more inner satisfaction than most people. Elaine and Steven loved her, she reminded herself. She should count her blessings, instead of crying for the unattainable!

Though Josh confused her with Joanna, she knew that, except in looks, they had been nothing alike. She had never understood Joanna's callous treatment of the people who loved her, especially their parents. After leaving home, she had returned to visit them only that one time with Josh.

She guessed that her sister had appeased her conscience by the duty letters she sent occasionally, brief strokes of ink on paper that did little to satisfy those she had left behind. It had been Diana who had remained to try and assuage some of the loneliness her parents felt without their beautiful Joanna, but she had always known she couldn't make up for the empty place at the table.

With a sigh, she turned and retraced her steps. She felt calmer now and more able to face what had to be faced. She realized that the dividing line between the insecure child of her past and the woman she was now was a thin one. Josh had undermined the self-confidence she had struggled so hard to develop over the years, and she could feel herself reverting once again to the little girl desperate to be valued for herself.

Any relationship with Josh was certain to follow the pattern of her previous relationships, she realized. With every stroke of his hands on her body, and every kiss on her hungry lips, she would wonder if it was she he touched, or if she was again being forced into becoming a substitute for her sister. She would never have the love from Josh she needed, but as she had done so many times before, she would settle for whatever she could get.

She would learn to take, as Joanna had, she vowed, and somehow, she would manage to maintain her own independence from him. Otherwise, she would be lost to any hope of being loved for herself, and instead, she would once again be trapped by her sister's image.

Diana opened the door as quietly as possible, with the hope of returning to her room undetected. She should have known better than to enter through the front door, she thought with exasperation, as Steven's voice called from the living room.

"Mama!"

Childishly she held her breath, her hand clenched on the knob.

"What are you doing?" Josh's mocking whisper caused her eyes to fly open in consternation.

"I'm not doing anything." She frowned at him. "Can't I even take a walk without having to endure a third degree?"

"The way you were standing with your eyes closed, it looked as if the only thing you were doing was trying to practice invisibility. There's no way to hide from what happened, honey."

She was on the verge of responding to his hateful drawl of amusement with anger but was prevented by the sound of Steven's voice. He was lying on his stomach before the fire, his lips petulant as he turned accusing eyes in her direction.

"Where was you?" he questioned, his face assuming a disapproving scowl. "I wanted to go with you!"

Knowing him almost better than she knew herself, she detected the quavering sulkiness in his voice that usually preceded a temper tantrum. Oh Lord! That was the last thing she needed now!

She went to walk past Josh, who seemed to take up an enormous amount of space.

"Don't walk away from me, Diana," he demanded, his eyes narrowing as he observed her harried expression. "Steven can wait his turn."

Her eyes flew to his face and moved to look over his shoulder at Steven. The child was pushing himself into a sitting position, his face mutinous as he observed her closeness to his father. Irritated at being ignored, Josh placed restrictive hands on her shoulders, and with the sensation of being caught in the middle of two opposing forces, she noticed the jealousy in Steven's eyes.

"Let me go," she hissed, trying to pry his fingers loose.

With one swift, sure movement, he pulled her resisting body against his and bent his head until his mouth was just inches away from hers. His warm breath fanned her mouth and sent a weakness through her traitorous body that left her gasping.

"Steven's watching." She forced her head backward as she made the protest and tried desperately to get away from that sensuous mouth and the craggy, fascinating face too masculinely attractive for her peace of mind.

"He's got to get used to the idea of sharing you, Diana." His murmured words held a wealth of sensual meaning. "You've got the boy so dependent on you that he almost went wild when you went out without him. It's time he learned that having a father means to him what it does to other kids. They have to share their parents with each other, and so must he!"

"But I'm not his mother!"

"You're the only mother he's ever known."

"And you're claiming the rights of a father? You have those rights over Steven, Josh. But don't imagine that I'm prepared to play the little woman in your life."

"Must it be a game, love?"

"I don't know what you're talking about."

"You will!" He released her, but his determined words remained between them. As much as she wanted to ignore their import, the conviction written across his features prevented her. Her face registered her fear, and with a sound of disgust, he turned.

"I'm not going to get anywhere while you're in this mood, am I? Go on, go to the boy! But in case you're wondering, I have no intention of letting you hide from me forever, Diana."

Biting her lip in bewilderment at his sudden capitulation, she stared after his retreating figure. As his footsteps carried him into the kitchen she breathed a sigh of relief. She walked over to Steven and repressed an impatient exclamation when she saw the accusation in his eyes.

"You like Daddy better 'n me." He lowered his head, his lower lip pushed forward sulkily.

"Steven, that's not true."

"It is too," he admonished, his eyes filling with tears. "I wanted to go with you!"

Going down on her knees beside him, she reached out and tenderly brushed the perpetually flopping lock of hair from his forehead, her mouth curving in amusement as the errant strands once again toppled forward. Josh's hair behaves in the same undisciplined manner, she thought. Appalled at the trend of her thoughts, she snatched her hand back and her own lower lip took on the same sulky curve as the child's.

"Steven, I thought you were happy playing with Daddy, that's why I didn't ask you to come with me." Her explanation sounded disjointed, her mind desperately trying to channel her thoughts away from Josh.

Frowning at her, his small forehead wrinkled in concentration as he considered whether or not to accept her explanation. With heartfelt relief she saw his face clear, and his usual sunny smile reasserted itself.

"See what Daddy made?" His earlier complaints were forgotten in his eagerness to show her his treasure.

"Why Steven, that's beautiful!" Diana's exclamation was sincere as she looked down at the small book Steven held in his hands. Taking it carefully from him, she turned the pages slowly, savoring the charm of the sketches that filled the paper. Josh had printed short, appropirate captions beneath each picture, and the book was wonderfully suited to a boy Steven's age.

"A big-boy book, Mama." His finger pointed to the character Josh had depicted. "See, he's just like me!"

The sensitivity and love that went into the book caught at her heart. She was so intent on studying it, she failed to hear Josh's return.

"How about rewarding me for my efforts, Diana?"

The eyes she raised to his were wary. "Do you need a reward, Josh?"

"Not really." His smile encompassed the glowing face of his son. "I thought you might enjoy having dinner with me tonight, that's all."

Nibbling at her lip, she began automatically shaking her head in a negative movement. "The night air's too chilly to take Steven out in, Josh." Seeing the defeated expression on his face, she quickly added, "But you can stay for dinner, if you'd like."

"Don't you think Elaine might be willing to play baby-sitter tonight?"

For you, she'd do anything! she almost retorted. Since the first day she had introduced her friend to Josh, Elaine had been totally enraptured. She couldn't blame her, she thought. Josh, sensing Elaine's need to be included in their lives, had smiled with real sincerity. "Since both Diana and I lack parents, I'm glad Steven hasn't been left out of having a grandmother," he told her. Even now, remembering the joy on the older woman's face, her own throat constricted with emotion.

"I don't . . ." Diana began.

"I don't think she'll find it much of a hardship, either. I'll give her a call, and phone for reservations while I'm at it."

As he turned and quickly made his way into the hall she glared at his back with frustration. Damn it! she mused. Didn't she have any backbone? Why did she let him maneuver her into doing exactly as he wanted? A wry smile curved her mouth. Because it's usually what you want, too, Diana! her inner voice whispered.

6

His grin was even more pronounced as he returned to join them in the living room.

"Elaine will be here in half an hour," he said. "That'll give me just enough time to run home and change."

"Where are we going, Josh? You seem to have more than a simple dinner in mind, and I'd hate to find myself inappropriately dressed."

He ignored the truculence in her voice. "Wear a dress, sweetheart. I'll enjoy seeing your legs."

His demand was accompanied by a suggestive leer, his eyes dancing at her outraged expression. Much to her disgust, she couldn't prevent the laugh that forced itself from her mouth. It was normally difficult to resist his potent brand of charm, she thought, but when he was in this ebullient mood, it was impossible!

As if possessed of a sudden excess of energy, Josh bent down to swing Steven high in his arms.

"You'll be good for your grandma, won't you, son?"

Diana withheld a startled exclamation, her eyes briefly meeting Josh's over the child's head. His face stilled, losing some of its animation as he waited for her reaction. With a shamed smile, she nodded.

As much as she loved Elaine and valued their friendship, it was Josh who saw Elaine's need to be a permanent part of their lives. Elaine had been the mother Diana had always longed for. She was upset with herself for not thinking of such a simple method of rewarding Elaine's devotion.

"She's not my grandma," Steven scoffed. "She's just Elaine."

"She loves you like a grandma, and that's all that matters," Josh corrected. "I think it would make her very happy if you called her grandma, don't you?"

Silently, Steven nodded. An engaging dimple peeped from the corner of his mouth. "When's my grandma coming, Daddy?"

Josh threw Steven in the air, and he giggled with a mixture of nervousness and delight. Lowering him to the floor, Josh patted his little bottom before straightening and turning in Diana's direction.

"She can't get here soon enough for me, son!"

Flustered from the glittering promise in his eyes, Diana hurried Steven into the bathroom. Josh yelled that he was leaving, and as the front door slammed shut behind him, her relief was enormous!

Her hands shook slightly as she quickly divested Steven of his clothing and ran the water in the tub. She didn't trust Josh in this mood, she realized. He was entirely too sure of himself, and of her!

After putting Steven in pajamas, she left him playing quietly on his bed while she hurried to prepare herself for the unexpected outing. A hot shower did much to restore her calm, and later she was lavish with the sweetly scented vial of perfume that she removed from the top of her dresser.

It felt good to be smoothing nylons over her slim legs. She had almost forgotten, during the cold winter months, what it was like to feel entirely feminine. She chose a blue wool dress, whose boat-necked collar emphasized the shadowed hollows of her slender neck. Not only was it attractive, but entirely appropriate, she decided. The long sleeves and thick fabric would insulate her against the cold outside, and yet the softly clinging material added a definite touch of voluptuousness to her slim figure.

Determined to be ready by the time Josh returned, she didn't bother putting her hair up. Instead she left the reddish brown tresses to swing silkily over her shoulders. By the time she was satisfied with her appearance, she had worked herself up to such a fever pitch of anticipation that she found it difficult to leave the familiar safety of her room. The ring of the doorbell provided the catalyst she needed, and with a deeply drawn breath she walked into the living room.

She ushered Elaine into the room and closed the door behind her before she turned to give her a welcoming hug.

"I'm sorry we didn't give you more warning. Josh is great for spur-of-the-moment decisions." She hoped

Elaine didn't notice the strain in her eyes, but apparently her acting ability was better than average, because Elaine only returned her embrace with a laugh.

"Yes, he's an impulsive devil, all right. But quite a man, wouldn't you say?"

Diana flushed, turning toward the closet in the hall with Elaine's coat over her arm.

"If you say so," she muttered, relieved when Elaine chose to stay by the warmth of the fire. "By the way, Josh has planned a little surprise for you."

She approached her friend as she spoke, placing her own coat over the back of the couch. At the inquiring quirk to Elaine's brow, Diana smiled and called for Steven.

He entered the room like a small tornado, hurling himself into Elaine's arms with youthful enthusiasm. She lifted him into her arms and tickled him under his chin.

"How's my big boy?" she teased, placing nibbling kisses on his cheeks. "I've sure missed you, you little pest. Have you been having a good time with Daddy?"

Steven wriggled out of her arms. Grabbing her hand, he demanded, "Grandma, come see my big-boy book."

Elaine's face whitened, her eyes filling with tears as she searched Diana's expression.

"That's the surprise I was talking about," she whispered, her own throat closing. "Do you mind?"

"Oh, honey!" Elaine straightened her shoulders, a look of pride and love entering her soft brown eyes. "I don't know what to say!"

Josh chose that moment to arrive. He entered the

room before either Diana or Elaine had a chance to respond to his forceful knock. At her first sight of him Diana caught her breath at the sheer male magnetism he exuded. Dressed in a dark blue vested suit of Italian cut and a paler blue open-throated shirt, he was casual but elegant, and totally devastating. His own eyes, busy with an appreciative survey of their own, had her reaching for her coat in embarrassment.

"You're lovely." His words were audible only to her as he helped her into her coat.

"Thank you. You look pretty good yourself," she said, stepping away from him and bending to kiss Steven good night.

"You two have a good time, and don't worry about getting home early." Elaine's voice followed them out of the door. "I only live down the road, and it'll do me good to keep these old bones up past ten o'clock."

Diana walked beside Josh, her booted feet negotiating the irregular path with difficulty. She didn't know whether or not to be relieved when a strong arm circled her waist, guiding her the last few feet to his low-slung Porsche.

"How did you know I dislike my women keeping me waiting?"

Even though she heard the teasing inflection in his voice, she still rose to the bait. Tossing her head disdainfully, she passed him with her chin raised and seated herself before favoring him with a reply.

"I'm not one of your women, so it doesn't apply to me, does it?"

Holding the door, he glanced down at her. She could see the enigmatic expression in his eyes by the interior light of the car. His murmured, "We'll see," caused her heart to pound, and her body tensed as he walked around and seated himself beside her.

She was anticipating a tongue-tied silence, but to her surprise it didn't occur. Josh put himself out to set the mood for their date. He mentioned the passing scenery, the cold purity of the weather, and soon she found herself chatting unconcernedly.

They drove to the Sahara Tahoe Hotel, and as he parked the car and helped her to alight she felt a vague disappointment. She wasn't one for gambling and bright lights and would have preferred the out-of-doors on such a beautiful evening.

"Why the long face?" he asked, taking her arm and leading her into the foyer.

"I . . . Oh, you're imagining things," she stammered, and refused to meet his eyes.

There didn't seem to be anything to say after that, and she felt uncomfortable as she walked beside him. She was grateful for the myriad people milling around them and even a little envious. They all acted as if they knew exactly where they were going, while she felt suspended in midair.

A puzzled frown crossed her face as Josh led her to the tourist information desk. Her frown turned to a delighted smile when she heard Josh making reservations for a cruise. Following the clerk's instructions about boarding, they were once again leaving the casino.

"Where does she go, Josh?" Her voice was excited, and she blushed when he turned to look at her with the indulgent smile he sometimes gave Steven.

"She's the M.S. *Dixie,* and we'll be taking a short cruise around the lake toward Emerald Bay. You seemed to enjoy our visit there, so I thought you might like a chance to see everything from the water."

"Oh, yes," she breathed, her eyes shining as the beautiful paddle-wheeler, three decks high and gleaming white in the sunshine, came into view.

The cruise was about two hours long and took them across Lake Tahoe and into Emerald Bay, where they had an offshore view of Vikingsholm Castle and Fannette Island. For the first time, Diana noticed a picturesque building on the small craggy earth rising from the azure waters. Questioning Josh, she discovered it was called the Teahouse.

After returning to shore, she felt sadness at having reached their journey's end. She had enjoyed the cruise, but it was Josh's company that had made the trip beautiful. At least there was still dinner to look forward to, and suddenly the rest of the evening stretched before her with golden promise.

"We could have dined on board," he remarked, after seating himself beside her in the car and starting the engine. "But I have something rather special planned, if your tummy can hold out for another hour."

"Mmmm, I'm game," she murmured contentedly.

His eyes raked her features, hooded lids hiding his thoughts. He was worse than a schoolboy on his first date, he thought in disgust. He had planned this evening for weeks, but now that the moment had finally arrived, he was suffering from a severe case of cold feet. He couldn't seem to prevent himself from acting like a lovesick fool and only hoped the childishness of his behavior didn't give Diana the idea that he was usually such a stupid oaf.

Glancing surreptitiously at the man at her side, Diana noticed a muscle pulsing in his jaw. At that moment he turned and caught her eyes on him. When he made no effort to return her smile as he turned away from her and exited the parking area, all of her newfound pleasure in his company left her, and she turned her own head to stare sightlessly out of the window at her side.

Josh traveled past South Lake Tahoe with confidence, but their earlier light conversation was missing. As they turned up Ski Run Boulevard she was fighting to hold back tears. They had been so relaxed only minutes ago, she thought, clenching her hands together in her lap. It made this new stress she sensed in him even more difficult to bear.

Walking beside him a few moments later, she could almost feel the wall between them, and much as she longed to reach out and bridge it she didn't dare. His expression forbade any familiarity, and she just didn't feel capable of facing a rebuff. When they had reached their destination at last, she looked around her with puzzled eyes.

To her surprise, they boarded a waiting tram. The new, unapproachable Josh didn't seem unduly worried about whether or not she wanted to accompany him onto a transport that looked none too secure but just silently helped her to seat herself.

As they started out, the tram lifted slowly, the small jerks it gave causing her to clench her fists in her lap.

She gave a start when Josh's hand covered hers with comforting pressure.

"Don't be nervous," he whispered, his hair brushing her cheek and making her flesh tingle. "There's no danger, only gorgeous scenery. The tram will climb to around two thousand feet, so you'll get a unique view of the Sierras as well as the lake below."

"W-what does it do, just stop and then go back down?" She knew her voice sounded quavery. She only hoped he would think it was a fear of heights and not his nearness that was causing her uneasiness.

As if he regretted their enforced intimacy, he straightened. "You'll see," he muttered, and removed his hand from hers abruptly.

His enigmatic remark was explained as the ride ended and all the passengers began to disembark. Following the crowd, she tried to ignore the feel of his hand at her elbow.

The air was thin and fine, and from their vantage point the scenery was, as Josh had promised, truly breathtaking. She could see out over the top of the Sierra mountains. Below, the green of the trees seemed to flow and merge into an undulating mass. She caught her breath and looked at Josh with the glory of the mountains reflected in her eyes.

"Come on," he said curtly, his hand again gripping her arm almost painfully. She was glad his head was turned away from her and that he couldn't see the pain of hurt disillusionment reflected on her face.

The rest of the outing, to her relief, remained rather impersonal, as they both attempted to behave with a calm it was apparent neither felt. They sat on a sun deck before dinner at the Top of the Tram Restaurant, which she hadn't even known existed, and sipped cocktails. More for something to do with her hands than anything else, she began feeding the chipmunks, which were so tame they came right to the table.

The antics of the small animals didn't lessen the growing tension between herself and Josh. She was becoming more and more uncomfortable, and then he made a sudden exasperated movement in her direction.

"Let's go in to dinner."

She hardly tasted the beautifully prepared food. She was too aware of the brooding expression on his face and the fleeting glances he sent in her direction throughout the meal. To give him his due, he did try to put her at ease, but his attempts at conversation were somehow stilted, and she found herself having difficulty responding. She felt only relief when they left the dining area.

The velvet silence of the night greeted them as they moved in the direction of the tram. She avoided looking at him and was startled when she heard him utter a muffled oath. Before she knew what was happening, he had pulled her into the shadows, his arms jerking her against his taut body.

"I need this!" he groaned as his mouth descended to hers. For what seemed an eternity his lips learned the soft contours of hers. By the time he raised his head, she was shaking with the same longings she sensed in him.

The euphoria she felt in his arms was abruptly ended as she finally made sense of the frantic words breathed against her neck.

"You've got to belong to me, sweetheart. I can't take much more of this!"

"Do you think it's any easier for me?"

As she admitted the truth to both him and herself she pressed her face against the soft material of his vest.

"Then marry me, love," he said softly, giving her no chance to reply as his mouth again captured hers. She stiffened in his arms. She hadn't expected his proposal, only his seduction. Now she understood the reason for his behavior, she thought dully. He hadn't, as she had assumed, been displeased with her. Instead, he had been preparing himself for the moment when he asked her to become his wife.

Pulling away from the warmth of his body, she kept her eyes lowered to his chest as she mumbled, "Josh, I can't. . . ."

Gentle fingers traced her mouth. "I promise you won't regret it. I know I'm not much of a prize, but I'll do my best to make you happy."

The sun was beginning to set as they began their return journey. Again there was silence between them, although Josh's arm now circled her shoulders in a closeness she found stiflingly possessive. She knew that he was interpreting her silence as acceptance of his proposal, and she hated herself for not uttering the refusal she knew she must give.

She couldn't marry him! As the thought tortured her with its finality, she knew the bitterness of regret like a leaden weight in her heart. She loved him so much, but she knew it wouldn't be long before jealousy of the past turned that love to hate. She couldn't find solace in being his wife, in giving him her future and allowing it to be twisted by the love he had shared with Joanna. She knew herself incapable of handling marriage with a man who didn't love her for herself. Who only sought, through her, to revive a beloved ghost.

During the drive home, and later after Elaine's cheery departure, she tried to find a way to word her refusal. Each time she was prevented from succeeding by the subdued glow in his eyes.

"I . . . I'll just go and check on Steven."

Sensing her confusion, he only nodded, and she turned into the darkened hallway. Her body felt drained from all the emotional shocks she had undergone since morning, and she felt, as she tucked the tumbled covers around the sleeping child and bent to kiss him good night, that she couldn't take much more.

Longing for her own bed and the sweet forgetfulness of sleep, she closed Steven's door.

"Diana?"

She wasn't surprised at hearing Josh's whisper. Hadn't it been there between them since that episode earlier, this awareness that seemed to leap between their bodies at unguarded moments. Oh God! Was it just a few hours ago that she had been in his arms, held close to the pulsing hardness of his body?

As he approached she stared at the softly curling hairs peeping from the open throat of his shirt. With a sensation of despair, she felt his arms enfold her, but she didn't resist when he pulled her closer. She laid her head against his chest and almost laughed at his quiver of surprise.

Now she knew how Steven felt when he nestled

against his father, she thought inconsequentially, her eyes closing in contentment. His body was so warm, and the pounding of his heart was a soothing cadence beneath her ear.

Without protest she allowed him to lead her into the shadowed warmth of her room and stood silently even when he firmly closed the door behind them. With quick movements he undressed her, and again she uttered no protest.

The moonlight filtered through the undraped glass, sending dancing reflections over the gleaming Swedish wood of her dresser. What was she doing here, standing naked in front of this silent man, whose eyes seemed to devour her?

"God, you're beautiful," he breathed as he lifted her and lowered her gently onto the bed.

Closing her eyes as he drew the covers around her, she sighed as the warmth spread through her aching body. This is what she had longed for, she thought, concentrating on the sounds he made as he undressed. She felt his weight depress the mattress, and then he drew her into his arms with all the gentleness she could ever have wished for.

Her head rested beneath his chin, and even as she turned to place her lips against the strong column of his throat she knew they had reached a turning point in their relationship, one that would probably cause them both anguish. As soon as the first doubt arose in her mind others followed fast and furiously, and even though she ached to remain in his arms, she began to struggle.

"Just relax, honey. You'll get used to the feel of me in your bed before long. This is just the first of all the nights of our lives together."

At the huskily muttered words, she closed her eyes and swallowed convulsively. Josh uttered a muffled laugh, and she tensed as one masculine finger traced the rigid contours of her cheek.

Dear Lord! One proposal of marriage, and I completely lose my mind, she thought. She remembered standing in the hallway with the comforting warmth of his hard chest beneath her head, her arms clutching his solid back as if she would never let go.

What in the world was **she** going to do? she wondered in frustration. After practically dragging him to her bed, did she just smile and say, "By the way, Josh. I know you took my silence for agreement, but I really meant to tell you no when you asked me to marry you?"

As his finger moved to circle the soft flesh below her ear she shivered, closing her mind to the sensations he aroused. Her mental exhaustion was no excuse. She could have stopped him before now if she had really wanted to, but that was the problem. Why else would she have stood so docilely while he undressed her?

She cringed from the memory of her submissiveness, but what was even more disturbing was recalling her reaction when he had looked at her afterward. His eyes had feasted on her naked flesh, and at the picture her mind formed a hot flush spread over her skin, deepening when she realized that her heightened color wasn't due entirely to embarrassment but also stemmed from the arousal engendered by the memory.

Disgusted by her own weakness, she decided it was not too late to call a halt to Josh's lovemaking. She would stop him even if she had to accuse him unfairly of taking advantage of her tiredness. But as her glance locked with his the words just wouldn't come.

In his eyes, she saw his awareness of the soft, quivering flesh hiding under the covers, which were all that separated them. With sure movements his hand stroked the nervous pulse beating in her throat and slid down until he gripped the edge of the sheet she held. He pulled it from her tightening fingers with little effort. She protested, reaching down to retrieve the crumpled sheet.

"Don't!" His voice was a pleading groan. "I want to look at you."

His eyes moved from her face to the delicate contours of her neck. Her body pulsated with life, and she was stunned by the intensity of her arousal. She knew he felt the wildness in her. His awareness was there in the eyes that stared in fascination at the increasingly violent pulse pounding in her throat.

Slowly, Josh's head moved down until his lips covered that telltale beat, and she couldn't suppress a moan of pleasure at the warmth of his lips against her flesh. At the sound, his body tensed and one hand moved up to her shoulder.

Raising himself on his elbow, he slid his other hand beneath her neck, and his fingers tangled sensuously in the soft hairs curling at her nape. His eyes continued their leisurely exploration, until they reached her rounded breasts. A shudder convulsed him as he noticed the pink nipples hardened in passion.

"Touch me!"

"L-let me get up, Josh."

"Why?" he questioned, impatiently. "I want to feel your hands sliding over my body, honey. I'm as hungry to have you learn what pleases me as I am to please you."

With purpose firming his mouth, he slid his hand caressingly across her shoulder until his hand clasped her own.

She closed her eyes, biting her lip in an effort to lessen the sensations shooting from her fingertips as he forced her hand against his flesh.

"That isn't so difficult, is it?"

She clutched at the soft hairs on his chest to try to still the sensuous exploration, only to release them as she heard his moan of arousal.

Moving swiftly, his body rolled to cover hers. As he levered himself on his elbows his large hands tangled in her hair, and he lowered his mouth to hers with hungry intensity.

She moved to push at his firm shoulders, but somehow her intention was confused by the feel of his skin against her palms. With a groan of surrender, her arms instead slipped around his neck. She was beyond reason, given over to feeling, and the things he made her feel were wonderful!

Their breathing was harsh in the quiet dawn, but it only added an intensity to their lovemaking. She gasped as his mouth moved across her face to her neck, and she arched her head to encourage the exploration of his lips.

"I want you so much." His aroused cry was muffled against the sensitive hollow beneath her ear, his warmly abrasive tongue sending shivers through her as it circled the lobe. His body slid against hers in urgent rhythm, the hard evidence of his arousal pulsating against her stomach. "Tell me you want me, too."

Without hesitation, she whispered, "I want you so much it hurts."

"Then let me soothe the ache in both of us, sweetheart," he gasped, and his legs parted hers, disregarding her momentary resistance. The brilliant glitter in his eyes was softened by a tender smile, his urgency temporarily controlled. He took the time to run his hands slowly along the inside of her thighs, moving higher with every stroke.

She cried his name as the pads of his thumbs sought and parted the apex of her need.

"Slowly, honey . . . slowly."

The breathy whisper temporarily soothed, then newer and more devastating sensations shook her. She gripped the tangled sheet, a series of strangled breaths matching the rhythm of her aching hips. His hands slid under her to knead her soft flesh. As he lifted her to facilitate the erotic roving of his mouth she twisted in an agony of frustration.

A low growl accompanied the passage of his tongue as it swirled a return pattern over her stomach and breasts, finally coming to rest inside her mouth. She clutched at the shoulders poised above her, her pleasure heightened by the taste of her own body clinging to his lips.

Suddenly impatient to capture the prize, his hips arched in renewed demand, and he took possession of her, hesitating only momentarily before resuming the age-old rhythm of love. Her growing delight obliterated a brief attack of conscience, and reality spun away and disappeared as her whole being dissolved in ecstasy.

7

~~~~~~~~~~~~~~~~~

Diana was awakened by water running in the shower. She frowned, for the moment disoriented, until she heard Josh's deep laughter and then a squeal of enjoyment from Steven.

From the racket they were making, it looked as though they were going to be spending quite some time mopping the bathroom floor, she thought, smiling. Rolling onto her side, she glanced at the clock. She groaned as much at the stiffness of her body as at the lateness of the hour. Then she furrowed deeper into the pillow's downy softness and closed her eyes to shut out the accusing hands on her alarm.

Pushing the blankets aside, she shivered as cool air touched her naked body. She pulled her thick golden velour robe over goose-pimpled skin and raised the front zipper until it rested securely against her throat.

111

She slid her feet into soft mules and moved to the dressing table. Staring disbelievingly into the mirror, she flushed. She had anticipated looking like something the cat dragged in, but what she saw was a woman who had been made love to very thoroughly in the night!

Her mouth was relaxed and slightly swollen, her eyes soft, as she slowly dragged her brush through hair tangled by Josh's hands. Her last memory was of nestling her cheek against his shoulder, while he tucked the covers around them both. She experienced again the drowsy aftermath of their lovemaking and held her breath as she remembered his voice soothing her into slumber.

"Sleep in my arms, my love."

Carefully she replaced the brush on the dresser top. "My love!" But she wasn't his, and she certainly wasn't his love, she thought. She refused to meet her eyes in the mirror, afraid of what she would see reflected there.

She didn't want to look inward, she realized. From the day of their first meeting, when Josh had glanced from her to Joanna without giving in to the impulse to remark on their resemblance, he had endeared himself to her. Joanna had slipped her arm around Diana's waist and glanced coyly across the space dividing them from her husband.

"Aren't we like two peas in a pod, sweety?"

Other than a momentary flinching of her facial muscles, Diana had given no sign of her painful shyness as she met the candid gaze of her sister's husband. He seemed to be seeing her clearly, without being blinded by Joanna's presence. He seemed to recognize her as the person she was, not simply a copy of her sister.

She had stared at Josh in growing wonder. A tremulous smile curved her mouth, and she caught her breath at the tentativeness of his answering grin. Without words they communicated something of their inner selves. He was no stranger, this silent man with the gentle blue eyes. He was a friend, a soul mate, and she was moved by their communication of spirit, until Joanna's grating laugh spoiled the moment.

"Get that look off of your face, sister dear," she drawled, the teasing inflection in her voice contrasting with the hardness of her glance. "He's all mine!"

"Don't be ridiculous, Joanna!" Josh's voice harshly answered his wife, his mouth curling in obvious disgust at her jealousy. Glancing again at Diana, he took her hand in his, stilling its tremor with the tightness of his grip. "Hello, little sister!"

He had done everything in his power to alleviate Diana's humiliation, but Joanna had achieved her purpose. From then until the day they left, Diana had never felt comfortable in Josh's company. She had been suitably chastened for the unwilling attraction she had felt for him.

At that time she had placed Josh on a pedestal; he was a dream too far out of reach ever to become a reality. Maybe that was why she had so readily believed that the man she thought she knew had been a figment of her imagination. By hating him, she eased the guilt caused by the attraction she felt for her sister's husband. His return had changed the dream to reality, she thought, but she closed her eyes as she railed silently against the unfairness of the guilt she was feeling.

Her mouth and body still retained the feel of his. She

could see them the way they had been in the darkness, their bodies moving together urgently, giving and taking pleasure. But the beauty of the memory brought only anguish, as she visualized Joanna standing beside them with bitter accusation in her eyes.

Her previous lightness of spirit was gone as she left the bedroom that would never again be her sanctuary. Josh had placed his mark on every inch of space.

Stumbling into the kitchen, she splashed her face with cold water. She pressed the towel against her skin for long moments, trying desperately to scrub away her depression. Oh, God! she thought. Now she was really in a mess. He was expecting more of her than it was possible for her to give, and she dreaded the moment she would have to tell him how she felt.

She worked with mechanical precision as she prepared breakfast, trying to keep her fears at bay. At first she was able to concentrate on the tasks at hand. Until she set the table for three. As she stared at the extra place setting, she struggled to hold back tears.

All the insecurities she had ever felt because of Joanna rose up to haunt her. Turning abruptly, she clutched the edge of the sink, breathing deeply to try to control her childish panic. With trembling fingers she reached into the cupboard, withdrew a coffee mug.

She realized that she was quickly becoming her own worst enemy. It wasn't Josh she was afraid of, but herself. She simply couldn't face a future in which she had to struggle to establish her identity as she had in the past. She remembered the way he had guided her body so gently hours before and winced. Even at the height of her pleasure, his whispered words of love and desire had caused her to break free of the sensuous spell he wove long enough to wonder if he was making love to her because he couldn't have Joanna.

Was she just a substitute for her sister, as she had been only a reminder to her parents of their beloved firstborn? She should be familiar with the pain of that old rejection by now, she thought bitterly.

All her life her parents had compared her to Joanna, never recognizing her as a person in her own right. She had loved them, and the loving had weakened her own independence. She had tried desperately to be whatever they wanted, but she knew she hadn't succeeded. She couldn't risk such a failure with Josh, she would be sure to disappoint him if she became his wife. Because now, she realized, she didn't even want to try to be like Joanna.

She was buttering the last slice of toast when Josh's arms circled her waist.

"Mmmm," he murmured, nuzzling the side of her neck. "This kitchen smells like heaven to a starving man."

"Everything's nearly ready." She was proud of the firmness of her voice as his body heat penetrated her robe and brought with it a resurgence of desire. "Why don't you sit down?"

"On second thought," he growled, his teeth nipping the lobe of her ear, "you smell even better. If it weren't for a certain young man who insisted on dressing himself, I'd take you back to bed and make a meal of you."

"I'd probably give you indigestion." Her reply was accompanied by a dismissive shrug, and his arms fell from her waist as she moved to lift crisp strips of bacon onto a draining rack. Placing them in the oven to keep warm, she broke several eggs in a bowl and began whipping them with a vengeance.

"Have I displeased you, or is it the eggs that have earned your wrath?"

Spreading the mixture into a buttered pan and adding seasoning, she snorted inelegantly. "Don't be ridiculous!"

"Strange," he said musingly, and moved to lean against the counter so that he could study her profile. "Last night, I was under the impression the pleasure was mutual."

"You know it was."

"Then why the frosty reception this morning?" he questioned, lifting a finger to trace the blush rising in her cheek. "Don't tell me you're shy!"

She jerked away from his touch as if scalded and turned resentful eyes in his direction. "It's not shyness," she retorted, ignoring the amused tenderness in his gaze. "For heaven's sake, you're not the first man I've slept with!"

He nodded, his eyes losing much of their earlier animation. "I'm aware of that, but it has nothing to do with us, does it?"

Lowering her eyes, she tipped the fluffy golden eggs onto a warmed platter. Suddenly, she saw a way out of her commitment to Josh and hoped, as she carefully thought out the lie, that Josh wouldn't notice the betraying pulse pounding in her throat.

"I'm sorry, Josh, but I think it does."

Total silence met her declaration, and beads of nervous perspiration dotted her upper lip. She held her breath, waiting for the explosion. To her surprise, it never came. Instead, his hand gently cupped the back of her neck, his fingers steadily massaging the corded muscles.

"What happened?"

"What usually happens? One minute I thought we were in love, and the next we were avoiding each other. Isn't there an old saying that fits, about something being 'wonderful while it lasts'?"

"You must have been very young."

Biting her lip, she nodded. Grasping the coffeepot she reached into the cupboard and provided him with a cup before turning to fill her own. "I was eighteen."

"For God's sake, how does something that happened when you were barely old enough to know your own mind affect us now?"

Here was the anger she had expected earlier, but now it took her by surprise. Staring down at the cup cradled in her hands, she thought carefully before replying.

She uttered a forced laugh. "Gilbert vowed undying love for months, until Joanna returned home from a modeling assignment. I couldn't blame him," she whispered dully, ignoring Josh's muffled imprecation. "Don't get me wrong," she insisted, turning her head until their eyes met. "Joanna never for one moment encouraged him. She didn't have to."

He heard the acceptance in her voice with a feeling of rage, curiously mixed with pity. He could almost see

Diana as she had been then, hurt, bewildered, and quite unable to compete with her sister's potent brand of charm. She was right not to blame that stupid idiot she had cared for, he thought. The poor sap hadn't stood a chance, any more than he had when Joanna decided she wanted him.

Was it simply Diana's loving nature that had prevented her from seeing the nearly imbalanced jealousy Joanna directed toward her? he wondered. He had sensed the tension between the two sisters from the beginning, and when he was introduced to Diana, he had felt intense compassion over the ambiguity of her position in her home. Certainly he had understood her hurt when Joanna openly encouraged their parents' obvious preference for her. He had been able to understand Diana's bewilderment, since Joanna had often used her attractiveness to other men to make him feel the same way. But remonstrating with his wife had only made matters worse, he remembered.

"What's the matter, Josh?" she had taunted, sitting cross-legged on the bed in their room. "Do you find my little sister appealing?"

"Don't be crude, Joanna," he muttered, moving to stand by the billowing curtains at the single window of the rather stifling room. Even with his back to her he could imagine her pose, one white and slender arm raised as she wielded a brush through her hair, her mouth twisted with a petulance he was finding more and more difficult to bear as the months passed and her boredom and dissatisfaction with their marriage became apparent.

"Why should the truth be crude, husband dear? After all, you only married me to get me into bed. Diana looks enough like me to satisfy your manly urges, doesn't she?"

"For God's sake," he muttered, disgust evident in his voice as he leaned his head against the window. "I don't remember having much difficulty getting you into bed. I married you because I loved you and at the time, you insisted that you returned my love."

"Even I'm allowed one mistake."

He shook his head tiredly. "There is a solution, you know."

"You'd like that, wouldn't you?" she sneered. "That would leave you with a clear conscience. You'd be able to preserve your self-righteous morality while lusting after my sister."

"Is nothing sacred, Joanna? Must you tarnish everything with your spite, even our marriage?"

"Our marriage!" She spat the words through gritted teeth, after flinging the brush violently across the room. "I'm sick to death of our marriage. You caress your typewriter keys with more fervor than you do me. I bet if little Diana was your wife, you'd spend more time in bed!"

A forbidden image entered his mind at that moment, of gentle, loving eyes bending closer . . . closer. . . . He swung violently around to face Joanna, and she smiled complacently as she noted the self-loathing in his eyes.

"She's the dull-little-woman type you wanted me to reduce myself to, isn't she?" Her whisper reminded him of the hiss of a snake just before it strikes for the kill, and he winced as much from the imagery as from the distortion destroying the beauty of her face. "You sanctimonious bastard! At least I'm honest about my wants, which is more than you are. I saw the way you looked at her," she screamed, her emotions building toward the hysteria he dreaded. "You don't love me! You've never loved me!"

He had gone to her then and reassured her as he had so many times before. But even as he held her until her sobbing subsided, he had realized that a part of himself had broken loose and escaped the coils she kept tightened around him. It was aggravatingly predictable when her fury turned to an almost uncontrollable passion, but for the first time he had been able to hold himself aloof from her demands.

"Tell me how much you want me," she insisted, her eyes wild against the hectic flush of her cheeks. Her crimson nails had raked the skin of his back through his shirt, as she attempted to pull him onto the bed. "You'll never stop wanting me, will you?"

Even now, he shuddered at the memory of the vindictiveness he had seen in her eyes as he pushed her clinging hands from his body and left the room.

The moment Josh turned away from her to grip the edge of the sink, Diana's last hope fled. If just the mention of her name could cause the pain she saw, then what hope did she have of ever having his love?

"It's ironic, isn't it?" She couldn't prevent the bitter inflection in her voice, any more than she could hold back a choking sob when Josh turned to stare at her. "Gilbert loved me and turned to Joanna, while you loved Joanna and turned to me. In different ways, we're both loving scarred, aren't we?''

In a sense it was true, she mused. Although she was devastated by Gilbert's defection at the time, the pain of his loss ended so soon that she knew what she felt for him hadn't been love. She had simply been hungry to have someone of her own to care for and had convinced herself that he was the man of her dreams. How stupid she had been at eighteen!

What she felt for Josh bore no relation to that earlier, ephemeral sentiment Gilbert had generated in her starved heart. Maturity had added a depth to her emotions she neither sought nor wanted, and last night in Josh's arms, she had learned the meaning of complete physical satisfaction, something Gilbert's furtive fumbling had never taught her.

Although the wonder of it still lingered, there would always be a barrier between them. It was her mind that refused to open to Josh! Without that final giving, she knew she could not make a good marriage.

''At least you used the past tense when discussing my feelings for your sister.'' The grating sound of his laughter broke into her reveries. ''I guess we're making some sort of progress!''

Her mouth twisted cynically. ''Oh, yes! You loved Joanna once, Josh. The only problem is, you still do.'' She motioned him to silence when he would have interrupted. ''Look, I know you're a man of integrity, too much so to lie about your feelings for me. I know you think you love me, but all I really am to you is a link with the past. The sooner you accept that I'll never willingly add more difficulties to an already unbearable situation by marrying you, the better off we'll be!"

"The only thing I accept is that for all your talk about believing in my integrity, you still think I'm a liar."

She sighed in exasperation. "Why do you twist everything I say? You listen, but you don't hear me. You've convinced yourself that what you feel for me has nothing to do with Joanna, but you can't be sure. Just answer one question, will you? Do I, or do I not, look like her?"

"Superficially, yes, but I . . ."

"Then you can't be sure, any more than I can, whether your feelings for me are real, and you're cruel to persist. Gilbert's defection was bad enough, although I could accept his attraction to a beautiful, vibrant woman. But you're asking me to compete with a ghost, and I refuse to be used like that again. Gilbert whispered empty words of everlasting love, but I shouldn't have believed him, any more than I should believe you now."

As he listened to her increasingly angry tirade Josh's face grew pale, deepening lines of stress running from nose to chin. Then he slammed his fist violently against the Formica counter, putting an abrupt end to her outburst.

"Damn it, Diana. I'm not about to let Joanna or some childhood affair come between us. We're good together, and that's not something either of us should take lightly."

"Sexually, yes," she whispered, turning her head to hide her pain at another lie. "But I like my life as it is, and I have no intention of marrying you, or anybody else!"

With a groan, Josh hauled her against him, and she felt the tremor that shook his strong frame.

"You haven't left me much of a choice." He sighed, smoothing her hair with gentle hands. "But be warned, Diana. I'm not used to being denied something I want this badly. I can't promise not to try to change your mind, but I'll give in for now."

Josh helped her transfer the oven-warmed food to the table and went to fetch Steven. As they returned together Diana's heart swelled with love and pride. They were both so handsome, these two men of hers, she thought. And Josh was her man, she realized. No matter what happened in the future, he would always be the lover of her heart.

After letting a fidgety little boy outside to play, she was collecting their plates with the idea of getting the washing-up out of the way when Josh interrupted her.

"I'll take care of these," he said, taking the plates out of her hands. "Why don't you and Steven come and spend the day at my place? The pool's open, and we can swim and laze around in the sunshine."

The invitation was a peace offering, and it was too tempting to refuse. She would be able to enjoy Josh's company with the security of having other people around. She nodded her acceptance before hurrying to dress. Donning corded slacks and a pearl-gray shirt-waist, she decided to forgo any makeup. She quickly piled her hair on top of her head and fastened it with a tortoiseshell clip. Then it only took her a few moments to unearth her cream bikini from the bottom of her dresser drawer.

Steven's summer clothes were packed away in a box in her closet. After lifting it down and laying it on the bed, she withdrew bright red swim shorts and a matching T-shirt. Eyeing the small garments, she shook her head dubiously. He'd grown so much over the last year, she only hoped they still fit him.

When she arrived at Josh's condominium, Diana changed Steven into his swim wear. Leaving him with his father, she went into the bathroom to take care of her own transformation. Eyeing herself in the mirrors, which appeared to be everywhere she looked, she flushed. Steven wasn't the only one who had gained a few pounds, she thought, resisting the urge to cross her arms over her breasts where they pushed upward against the material.

She rejoined Josh and Steven with her confidence lowered but not completely destroyed. Josh's blue eyes glinted knowingly at her approach until the ringing of the phone distracted his attention.

Josh had been on the phone for only a few minutes when she sensed something was wrong. Her heart sank as his lips firmed into a hard line, and her heart pounded in alarm as the color drained from his face.

The call was brief but had a devastating effect on his mood. As the hours passed, and they alternately swam or lay soaking up the sun on loungers, he seemed unable to completely hide his unhappiness. She didn't press him, instinctively understanding his need to come to terms with whatever it was that had upset him.

Josh sat on the edge of the pool, his hands clasped between his legs as he watched the glittering sparkles of late-afternoon sunlight reflecting off the water. Diana told him gently that she had to take Steven back to the house for his nap. When Josh began gathering their things together, she placed a sun-warmed hand on his arm.

"Bring them later, Josh. Why don't you stay here and unwind. While Steven rests, I'll start dinner, all right?"

"I was going to take you out to eat," he protested, albeit halfheartedly.

She smiled, her eyes crinkling defensively against the glare of the lowering sun. "Afraid I'll poison you?"

He shook his head, while his finger traced the golden bloom of her flushed cheek. Her eyes closed briefly at his touch. The gesture had him struggling against the lump forming in his throat. When she turned and grasped a protesting Steven by the hand, he wanted to call her back, to keep her warm concern for just a moment longer.

Josh was grateful for Diana's understanding. That phone call had shaken him, and he was finding it difficult to ignore the memories of the past it had stirred. To hear Ann's voice again, after all these years! At one time she and her husband Bob had been his best friends, during the days he had desperately needed friendship. But he had destroyed their relationship, through his insane suspicion and jealousy!

Even now, he winced at the memory of Bob's face as he accused him of abusing his trust by having an affair with Joanna. There had been anger, incredulity, and another emotion which at the time he hadn't understood. It was only later, when he discovered how wrong he had been, that he realized it was pity.

A few weeks later Bob had sold their home in Chicago and moved his family to California. At first he had seen the move as an effort on Bob's part to keep the truth from Ann. It had only been much later, when Joanna admitted she had lied to make him jealous, that he realized how wrong he had been. But by then it was too late for apologies.

That had been the night that the thin fabric holding their marriage together had finally burst wide apart, he remembered. Joanna had been packing to leave him, and he had been too stunned by the taunting viciousness of her words to make any attempt to stop her.

"Why, Joanna?" he muttered, his mouth a taut line against the whiteness of his face. "Were you trying to hurt me by hinting that my best friend was putting the make on you?"

"I never liked him or that sanctimonious goody-goody wife of his." She laughed, swinging around to face him with her hands on her hips. "In your mind you were always comparing me to her; don't bother trying to deny it. What I did served a twofold purpose. It removed your friends from my life, and it also brought you back to me, at least for a while."

"Then why are you leaving me, if our relationship matters so much to you that you'd lie to keep it?"

"Because I'm tired of being made to feel second rate," she snapped, her eyes filling with tears which she refused to let fall. "I can't be the wife you want, and trying to live up to your expectations is destroying me. Any love you once felt for me died a long time ago, and nothing I do is going to bring it back again. You can't give me what I need, and I can't live without something for myself."

"For God's sake, Joanna! I've never considered you second rate, but that is the way you view yourself, can't you see that? Maybe if we got professional help, we might be able to save our marriage. Would you be willing to try?"

A hectic flush of rage dotted her cheeks, and she snapped the lid of the suitcase shut in a single, violent motion.

"Are you saying I need a psychiatrist?"

"Of course not," he said, averting his eyes. "I only meant . . ."

Her movements were jerky as she moved toward the door; fingers bloodless from her grip on the handle of the suitcase she carried with her.

"There's nothing wrong with me," she screamed, flinging open the door and turning to glare at him with malevolence. "This is all your fault," she whispered, her eyes taking on an opaque vagueness that upset him more than her words. "You'll be sorry. Somehow, I'll make you sorry!"

As he rose and collected damp towels and depleted tubes of sun cream, he sighed. Joanna had achieved her aim. He had been hurt almost beyond bearing.

The wrong he had done his friend had been very real, something that had bothered him for a long time. Before accusing Bob he should have taken into consideration Joanna's mental state, but the possessiveness of his nature had at the time precluded rational thinking.

Now he had the chance to explain, to apologize to a man who had proved over and over again that he was a friend, and although he was going to take that chance, he dreaded the confrontation. Bob and Ann belonged to his past with Joanna, and his relationship with Diana was too shaky to be burdened with a tangible reminder of his life with her sister.

What an ironic twist of fate, he mused, his sandaled feet moving across the curving path with deliberation. Considering the size of the state of California, it seemed the oddest coincidence to find himself living within a few miles of Bob and Ann. According to Ann, she had just discovered his whereabouts from John, the agent who had first introduced them. Her voice had been openly eager, without any undercurrents of the hostility he might have expected.

"Promise you'll join us for lunch tomorrow, Josh? Bob and I can't wait to see you again."

He had been totally unprepared for the invitation, although later, remembering Ann's warmhearted generosity toward him in the past, he realized he should have expected it. With a terseness he was now ashamed to remember, he explained the existence of his son and Diana. When she extended the invitation to include both of them, he had had little choice but to accept.

"I'm so happy for you, Josh," she exclaimed. "And Steven's aunt, is she . . . nice?"

He winced at the hesitancy in her voice, knowing she was remembering the many times Joanna had been rude to her.

"She's more than nice," he remarked quietly. "You two will love each other."

8

~~~~~~~~~~~

They had traveled several miles the next afternoon before Diana finally accepted the inevitable and began to unwind. From the moment Josh had casually mentioned visiting his friends, she was beset by uneasiness. He hadn't listened to her protests and eventually she agreed to go, sensing that he needed her to be with him.

To her relief, Josh seemed content to chat with Steven as he drove and let her enjoy the passing scenery. The incredibly beautiful view made her forget her nervousness about meeting Josh's friends. She looked down at the river, swollen with snow melting from the mountains and tried to imagine the sounds it created on its journey, as it rippled over rocks and boulders and dashed itself against the steep sides of the riverbank.

She felt as though she were in that river. She felt a strong sense of rushing, rumbling currents carrying her along on their tide, whether she wanted to go, or not. There didn't seem to be any way to stop the flow. She would only end up dashed against the strong obstinacy of Josh's will if she tried. What bothered her most, though, was her growing uncertainty as to whether or not she had the strength to stop the progress of events.

Reaching North Lake Tahoe's center, she tried to answer the questions tormenting her. She was oblivious to the charm of the chalets nestled against the massive evergreens, their often garishly painted fronts looking somehow right in the year-round holiday atmosphere of the area.

As they passed quaint shops, which managed to retain an old-world charm amidst bustling business, she tried to restore some kind of order to her rambling thoughts. There was no point in lying to herself, she decided. Like the rushing river, she was being compelled to flow toward her destiny, even though she hated the helplessness she felt.

The possibility of eventually drowning from the torrent was very real. By feeding the raging longings she had kept bottled up for so long, Josh was becoming the mainspring of her existence, she realized. Though loving him meant pain, it also meant a strangely burning excitement, to which she feared she was quickly becoming addicted.

Josh turned the car onto a side road which began a gradual descent toward the shores of the lake. The trees overhead were tipped with glorious color as the brilliant afternoon sun delicately gilded the shimmering leaves.

Nervous perspiration wet her palms when they pulled into a graveled clearing. A large, rambling home glistened in sunlight that filtered through the dense shade of large graceful trees. A white, New England–cottage style house with green trim, it rested within twenty feet of the lakeshore, and she noticed absentmindedly that his friends had their own mooring dock, with a sleek and gleaming power cruiser tied up beside it.

She had just descended from the car and taken a deep breath of crisp, clear air, when they were hailed by a lilting squeal.

"Josh, we were beginning to think you weren't going to make it!"

Diana stood frozen in shy immobility while a petite blonde hurled herself down the front porch and into Josh's outstretched arms. When this small human dynamo turned welcoming hazel eyes upon her, Diana relaxed for the first time that day.

Diana turned to take Steven's hand while Josh made the introductions, when from around the corner of the house raced two freckle-faced boys and one large, floppy-eared dog. Skidding to a halt, the trio stared in their direction with irrepressible curiosity, two dirt-encrusted faces bearing identical grins, while the third member of their party sat on his haunches with head cocked and tongue lolling.

"As much as it shames me to admit it, considering the way they look," Ann said, laughing in the direction of the two boys, "they belong to us. The tallest is Kenny, and the husky fellow without his front teeth is Mark. Boys, this is Josh, an old friend of ours, and his son, Steven. And this is a new friend, Diana."

After the boys shook hands with amusing politeness, Josh turned his head, his eyes traveling from Kenny and Mark to their mother. "They were just babies the last time I saw them," he remarked, sadness in his eyes.

Ann's voice gentled with understanding. "Yes. It's been much too long, Josh."

"Do children always grow this fast? Why, they're practically men already."

Two thin chests in identical Superman T-shirts swelled with pride, and Diana quickly lowered her head to hide a smile. Josh just earned undying devotion with that one, she thought. She made a desperate effort to subdue threatening laughter but almost lost the battle when her eyes met those of the children's mother, who obviously shared her own lack of decorum.

"Boys, will you watch Steven while we visit? Take him with you and play cowboys, or something."

"Aw, Mom! We're being pirates today," Mark protested, voicing the disgust only a five-year-old can project. "Hey, Steve! You want to help me and Kenny dig for buried treasure?"

At the word "dig," Steven's eyes glinted with almost maniacal glee. Without hesitation he disappeared with Kenny and Mark, and Diana's amusement could no longer be contained.

"Oh, dear." She gulped, enjoying a shared moment of total communication with Josh.

His mouth quirking, he placed his arm around Ann, who was staring at them in puzzlement. As they turned to walk toward the house he explained his son's penchant for mountain building, and she giggled.

"I wonder how my two will like being bulldozers? I

can see it now. They dig, while Steven shapes the dirt into a mountain. What do you want to bet that before the day is out, the pirates become construction engineers?"

When introduced to Bob, Diana was once again enveloped in warmth and a feeling of family togetherness. He was of medium height, with light brown hair that curled in an engagingly boyish manner around his head. Though tanned and slimly fit, he didn't have Josh's sexual magnetism, although Ann might not agree with her, she thought.

Josh watched as shyly, unobtrusively, Diana endeared herself to both Ann and Bob. He had sensed their initial shock at her strong resemblance to Joanna, but within a short period of time her sincere pleasure in meeting them broke through any reticence they might have been feeling.

Already the two women were chattering together like old friends, and he felt warm satisfaction as he thought how right he had been. They had taken an instant liking to each other.

"We don't seem to be necessary to those two." Bob motioned with his head as his wife led Diana in the direction of the kitchen. "Why don't we take a drink down to the cruiser? Ann calls it my pride and joy, and she's not far wrong. I sometimes go there just to be alone and think."

"Sounds fine to me." While he watched as the drinks were mixed, Josh derided himself for the polite stiffness of his manner. Bob was making every effort to put him at his ease, and yet he felt none of the relaxed friendliness they used to share. Instead he was aware of too many things left unsaid, and sadness engulfed him when he remembered the way they used to discuss their hopes for the future.

A short while later, the two men were staring over the apparently limitless expanse of the lake with drinks in hand. An uncomfortable silence had come between them, and they both seemed to be at a loss to break it. Finally, Josh, seated next to Bob with his elbows resting on his legs, looked steadily at the swirling amber liquid in his glass and shook his head.

"I was a fool, but I guess you've always known that!" His voice was harsh. The one thing he wasn't prepared for was laughter, and as he heard the short, staccato sounds coming from Bob his body jerked upward in indignation.

"You find my efforts to apologize funny?"

"No." Bob snorted, ignoring the veiled warning in Josh's voice. "But I sure as hell fault your methods. If I agree with you, I'm admitting I always had a fool for a friend, and yet if I insist you weren't a blind, stupid idiot to believe that trash Joanna handed you, you might think there was some truth to her fantasies. I call that a no-win situation, old buddy!"

A tickling started somewhere in the region of Josh's chest, and soon they were both laughing uproariously.

"I should have remembered your penchant for irrational logic."

"And I should have remembered your damned stubbornness!"

They traded insults back and forth, both furiously

stretching the limits of their inventiveness. Each sally became more outrageous, and any strain that might have remained between them disappeared. Soon they were talking openly of Josh's relationship with Joanna, and the hell Josh had gone through after their separation.

"Bob, I would have given anything for your sanity," Josh admitted, his eyes holding those of his friend. "I was shocked when she walked out, but I should have been smart enough to see it coming. We didn't share the same dreams or interests, and yet I was too stubborn to listen when she tried to tell me. If I'd been more patient with her and tried to understand her needs rather than selfishly insisting that she be the one to compromise, it might have ended differently."

A sympathetic hand clutched his shoulder. "You couldn't have stopped her from going her own way, and you know it. I'd heard rumors, but I didn't want to be the one to lay any more trouble on your shoulders. That's why I understood your state of mind when we had that blowout. When you learned the truth, you could have reached me through John. Why didn't you?"

"You know the answer to that. I was too much a coward to call and apologize. I had blown our friendship royally and had to cut my losses."

"Why? Because you were loyal and tried to defend your wife? Hell! If Ann had even hinted to me that you'd tried anything with her, I'd have half killed you, and I wouldn't have waited for you to give me any explanations. You would have done the same, if deep down inside you hadn't known me better than to believe Joanna's lies."

Josh frowned, attempting to analyze his own past motivations. "You know," he muttered, shaking his head, "even before Joanna confessed her irrational reasons for destroying our friendship, I never hated you. If anything, I hated myself for missing you and Ann so much."

Bob's exclamation was accompanied by a wry grin. "You showed good taste!" He got to his feet, his teasing expression sobering as he slowly held out his hand in Josh's direction. "Friends?"

With a muscle pulsing in his jaw, Josh responded. "Friends," he rasped, the tightness of his grip revealing the depth of his emotions.

As Diana and Ann prepared a salad to accompany the buffet Ann had waiting for them in the dining room, they talked as if they had known each other forever. With burgeoning gratitude, Diana became aware of feeling that rare sense of inner closeness that marked the beginning of a firm friendship. Only with Elaine had Diana ever had such an instant and spontaneous rapport. She had been too shy to develop close friendships as a child and teenager, and her affair with Gilbert had only added to her reserve.

Thanks to Elaine's encouragement, she had just begun to break out of her shell and had even started accepting casual dates occasionally, when Joanna had shattered her brittle shell of confidence with her reappearance in her life. After that, there hadn't been either enough time or inclination to do more than survive. Her sister had been in such a depressed condition during her pregnancy that she could not be left alone for very long.

Later, after Steven was born, she had even less time for her single friends, and eventually they stopped asking her to accompany them.

She couldn't blame them. To be fair, it had been entirely her own fault. Elaine had often offered to watch Steven in the evenings, but she had wanted to spend every available moment alone with him.

"Shall we just carry this through to the dining room?" Ann asked, interrupting Diana's pensive mood.

Smiling, she followed Ann's bustling figure. The table looked delightful, and she felt a rush of gratitude for the effort Ann had put forth to welcome her into their home. There was a mouth-watering ham seasoned with cloves and a delectable-looking brown-sugar-and-mustard glaze, as well as turkey with all the trimmings.

"Ann, it must have taken you hours to prepare all this!" she exclaimed, her eyes moving from the food to the china place settings and shimmering crystal wine-glasses.

"Yes, it did." A roguish smile curved Ann's mouth. "But don't worry." She sighed, with just the right degree of self-sacrifice. "For the chance to meet you, I would have worked my fingers to the bone!"

"Humph! Before you start feeling sorry for this wife of mine, let me clue you in," Bob said, laughing, as he and Josh noisily entered the dining room. "Number one, she loves to cook, and number two, she loves to taste what she cooks. He smiled, slapping Ann irreverently on the bottom. "Usually by dinnertime she's so stuffed, she can't eat another bite. She tells me that way she can feel a wonderful sense of martyrdom when she passes up a meal."

"She doesn't need to pass up any meals," Josh murmured, a decidedly masculine appreciation in the eyes that roamed Ann's curves. "She looks pretty good to me!"

Ann blushed profusely and, with assumed indignation, told Josh to behave himself.

"Really, Diana," she continued. "I hope you're up to handling this lech."

Although Diana sent a warning glance in his direction, Josh deliberately ignored her silent message.

"Oh, she has her moments!"

"Boy, am I glad to find another woman who blushes," Ann said with heartfelt sincerity.

Josh and Bob both roared with laughter, while Diana silently fumed at the knowing looks they exchanged. Damn him! How in the world was she going to keep their relationship private, when he insisted on showing the world at large that they were a snug twosome? she thought, barely managing to hide her anger.

At the end of the meal, Bob opened a bottle of champagne. After filling their glasses, he proposed a toast to friendship. Diana was touched by the sincerity in his voice and briefly glanced at Josh as she lifted her wine.

She was dismayed by the possessiveness of his gaze, flushing hotly when she noticed the speculation in the glance Ann shared with Bob. When Josh's hand rose to boldly caress the back of her neck, she stiffened, rejecting his touch while resentment burned inside her.

He was staking his claim to her in front of his friends. A coldness spread through her as she realized that Josh was only biding his time until he increased her vulnerability to the point where she would give in to his demands. His attitude showed that her insistence upon living her own life meant less than nothing to his plans for her, and she couldn't allow it to continue.

There was only one way to convince him that they had no future together, and although her heart quailed at the prospect, he was giving her little choice. Somehow she would have to ease him from her life; the only question was *how*. After her response to his lovemaking, it wouldn't be easy to convince him that she felt nothing for him. If only, she thought, she could believe her own words about liking her life as it was!

Ignoring Ann's vociferous protests, she helped to clear the table before following the men outside. The activity eased some of her tension, and she was almost sorry when the last of the dishes were placed in the dishwasher. Later, as they sat sipping drinks on the wide, screened-in veranda that ran the length of the house she looked toward the placid waters of the lake, trying to lose herself in the startling blueness, needing to wipe out her increasing uneasiness in Josh's presence. Somehow the sigh of the wind through the trees and the glorious scenery surrounding them went a long way toward soothing the ache in her heart.

Summer was rapidly approaching, she realized, and the sunlight was quite warm. The snow of a few weeks ago had melted, and now there were only patches left on the ground.

"Do you think we'll have any more snow?" Diana asked, more for something to say than because of any real wish to know.

"There's always the possibility," Ann replied, "but I don't think it's likely. That storm we had in June last year was really freaky, wasn't it? Frankly, I've had enough of the winter. Like the boys, I'm a sun-worshiper."

"What about you, Diana?" Bob asked. "Are you a sun-worshiper too?"

"I guess I am, although I must admit I've enjoyed the snow. It makes everything seem so clean and pure."

"Then why did you keep yourself buried inside when Steven and I were building snowmen?" Josh inquired moodily.

It was obvious that Josh was becoming frustrated by her coldness toward him, but she stiffened her resolution. Her smile was perfunctory when she turned to answer.

"For one thing, I enjoy the snow most when I'm warm and snug inside." She watched the narrowing of his lids with assumed detachment. "Anyway, I felt it was a good opportunity for you and Steven to get to know each other."

"How about dessert?" Ann jumped up from the porch swing she was sharing with Bob.

Although Bob gorged himself on the pineapple torte Ann had prepared, Diana could only manage a small slice for courtesy's sake. Glancing surreptitiously at

Josh's plate, she noticed he wasn't faring much better. As evening approached, his terseness increased, and her head began to pound. Gratefully sipping the hot coffee Ann provided, she felt some of her discomfort subside, but the paleness of her face must have given her away.

"Are you all right?" Ann stopped her flow of chatter when she became aware of Diana's silence.

"It's nothing," she muttered, flushing with embarrassment when all heads turned in her direction. "Just a headache. I've been enjoying myself, and I didn't want to say anything to put a damper on the party. Forget it, please."

Diana knew she was talking too fast and allowed her words to trail off. She could tell by the sardonic expression on Josh's face that she was making a fool of herself, and she didn't need the swift glance Ann and Bob exchanged to affirm that fact.

"Daddy, Kenny and Mark wants me to stay and play." Steven's voice was followed by his hurtling figure as he threw himself into his father's arms. "Can I?"

Diana was just about to utter an emphatic no, but Josh sent an inquiring glance in Ann's direction. Ann was quick to offer to keep Steven overnight, promising to bring him home after dropping the boys off at school in the morning.

"He's big for his age." She smiled. "I'm sure Kenny's pajamas would fit him."

"Oh, boy!" Steven's eyes were wide with excitement as he glanced from Kenny to Mark.

Diana didn't miss the determination on Josh's face,

and she began to feel panicky. She didn't want to be alone with him tonight. She wanted to delay the confrontation she dreaded, at least until she had had time to think. But one glance at Ann's delighted expression left her mute, as Josh had known it would, she thought with resentment.

Diana felt awkward as they took their leave, but she did a good job suppressing the anger that threatened to explode inside of her.

Within minutes of waving good-bye, Steven was out of sight, trotting importantly after Kenny and Mark as if staying with strangers was something he did every day of his life. She couldn't prevent a few tears at his defection, but at the same time, she was proud that he was growing up. As she seated herself in the car she wiped away the embarrassing moisture clinging to her lashes.

While Josh was busy driving, she glanced in his direction and noticed the tautness of his mouth with trepidation. She resisted the urge to ask him to reduce his speed, stoically clutching the edge of the seat while she tried to ignore the climbing speedometer.

Josh turned to glare at her. As he noticed the expression on her face he lifted his foot from the gas pedal until the car had slowed.

"What's with you, Diana?"

"Since I'm not a mind reader, I haven't the least idea what you're implying."

"Oh, come on," he snapped, gripping the wheel tightly. "You did your damndest to cold-shoulder me in front of Ann and Bob."

"Maybe I did, but you deserved it. You were acting like you owned me, and I won't stand for it. I'm not your possession, Josh, and I won't have other people think I am!"

"Why? Because you want to be free to bat those eyelashes of yours at every presentable male?"

"Damn you, you're talking nonsense," she cried, shaking her head. "I can't be bothered batting my eyelashes at you or anyone else."

"Can't you, Diana? Isn't that really why you won't marry me, because you want to play the field?"

"Don't talk like this, Josh. You don't know what you're saying."

She didn't have much hope of making him listen, so she was surprised to hear his quiet apology. "You're right," he said, running his hand through his hair in agitation. "I don't know what the hell I was thinking of."

She wouldn't cry, she thought, biting her lip. She didn't know what was really bothering him, or why he was taking it out on her, and she didn't want to know. All she was concerned with at the moment was controlling her lacerated feelings, even though it took every ounce of willpower she had to do so.

There wasn't another word spoken between them as they continued the drive. All too soon they were turning into the approach to her home. She kept her eyes resolutely forward, her body held stiffly.

Walking up the path, she fought the urge to bolt. As she preceded him through the front door she avoided contact with Josh's body. But even so, she felt his presence as completely as if he touched her.

She took as long as she could to hang her coat in the hall closet. She looked at Josh warily as he watched her movements, his body casually lounging against the far wall.

Turning, she began moving toward the impersonal security of the living room, only to be stopped by his hand on her arm.

"Diana, I've said I'm sorry for acting like a jealous idiot. What more can I do to make up for my rotten behavior?"

Glancing into the remorseful blueness of his eyes, she saw pain mingle with a desperate longing in his gaze, but hardened herself to resist his appeal. She hated herself for wanting him in spite of the scene he had just created, and her own weakness only increased a brooding sense of injustice.

"Come on, love," he coaxed, brushing her mouth with the tip of his finger. "Give me a smile."

If he thought she was going to make it easy for him, he had another think coming! She felt no satisfaction at the realization that his actions were motivated by jealousy. She had given him no cause to be jealous, damn him!

"Do you really think turning on the charm will make up for your obnoxious behavior?"

"If you won't accept it in words, then let me show you how sorry I am."

His attempt to place his arms around her was the last straw. Breaking free of his hold, she muttered, "Why don't you just leave?"

"I'm not going with you in this mood!"

His eyes were aglow with an emotion difficult to identify. Then she recognized it for what it was. He was enjoying this! she thought, with a surge of exasperation. She faced him with clenched fists resting on her hips.

"You're beautiful when you're angry, do you know that?"

The soft murmur was accompanied by a definite twitch at the corner of his mouth, and with a muffled curse she spun on her heel.

"I'm going to take a bath!" She stomped indignantly in the direction of the bathroom. "I don't doubt that you'll do what you damn well please." She paused long enough to impale him with a mutinous stare. "Just don't think you'll find me accommodating!"

"Come to think of it, I could use a good wash myself," he drawled.

As he spoke he moved closer, and she found herself rigid with anticipation. She couldn't seem to will her legs to move even an inch, and by the time she felt his hands warm on her shoulders, the opportunity for retreat was lost.

"Why don't we shower together?"

The taunting suggestion was whispered against her throat, and she stirred in his arms. She shook her head and pushed against his chest in protest. A heated flush colored her cheeks a delicate pink, the rosy hue darkening when she heard his muffled laughter.

"I thought not!" He traced the heated flesh with a caressing finger before releasing her and turning away. "But don't try to convince me the idea doesn't appeal!"

With an inarticulate exclamation she left him standing there, all too aware that he had seen beneath her anger to the infuriating desire she felt to know again the gliding pleasure of his forceful body against her own.

9

~~~~~~~~~~

Diana closed the bathroom door and made sure she locked it behind her. Josh's knowledge of her most basic needs unnerved her, and she resented her inadequacy when faced with his confident sensuality.

Quickly turning on the bathwater, she took off the now hated dress, not caring that it fell in a crumpled heap at her feet. By now her thoughts were such a jumbled mass of conflicting longings that she was barely aware of removing her undergarments and stepping into the tub.

She soaped her skin gently, distressed that the bath was failing to calm her. Quite the opposite. Thoughts of Josh brought her tingling flesh to life, and she clenched her teeth in renewed anger at the realization.

She rinsed herself and let the water out of the tub. As she stepped out onto the bath mat, she felt her body sway as a blinding pain splintered through her temples. The mild headache of a few hours ago had worsened into a true migraine, and nausea churned her stomach.

She rummaged through the medicine cabinet with trembling hands. Yes, here it was . . . the medication her doctor had prescribed for the violent tension headaches she suffered after Joanna's death. Dr. Stark had told her the migraines were brought on by nervous strain. He had reassured her that the unaccustomed pain would disappear in a short period of time, and he had been right.

Thank goodness, she thought, as she shook two of the white tablets into her palm. Getting them past the constriction in her throat wasn't easy, but after two glasses of water she finally got them down. Now it would just be a matter of waiting until the medicine had a chance to take effect, she thought with relief.

With a faint moan she closed her eyes and groped for her old faded robe hanging on a hook in the corner. She wrapped herself in the familiar if unbecoming garment and pulled the cord snugly around her waist.

Gathering her clothes and damp towel from the floor, she threw the whole lot into the hamper. Even the muffled thud sent new pain shooting through her head, and she swallowed quickly to control the leaping of her stomach.

The pills had partially dissolved in her mouth, and she couldn't bear the acrid taste a moment longer. She brushed her teeth with difficulty, fighting dizziness as she bent over the basin. After rinsing her mouth, she straightened with a grimace. Her hair was curling riotously over her shoulders from the steamy air, and she looked about sixteen. The thought didn't do much to increase her self-confidence, but she didn't care at the moment. The thought of dragging a brush across her overly sensitive scalp was intolerable.

She entered her bedroom, trying to hide her condition from Josh. As he got up from the bed she avoided looking at him, but she should have known he would notice how strained and pale her face was.

"What's wrong, honey?"

Immediately he was at her side, his face concerned as he placed the back of his hand against her forehead. She couldn't prevent herself from closing her eyes to savor the coolness of his touch, any more than she could resist leaning against his chest as his arms closed around her.

"Your headache's worse, isn't it?"

She was too miserable to protest when he pulled back the covers of the bed and lowered her into a reclining position against the pillows.

"I'll be all right. Just let me sleep." She was objecting to the sure movements of his hands as they worked to untie the cord of her robe. She might as well have saved her breath, though, because before she knew it the garment was removed, and she was being rolled onto her stomach.

"Will you stop fighting me? Relax, for heaven's sake!"

His words were no less forceful for being whispered, and the hands pushing against her shoulders emphasized his determination to make her yield. Fighting him was as useless as trying to fight herself, and with a defeated moan she yielded.

"That's better," he soothed, as he gently brushed her hair from her nape.

Better? she mused. It was marvelous! His fingers roamed her body from her neck to her calves and back up again. Over and over he repeated the process, his probing hands seeking and finding the tension points beneath knotted muscles.

The sickening throb continued at her temples, but it no longer mattered. Nothing mattered but hard hands stroking her body, and she squirmed her enjoyment when those very hands, no longer content with the smooth curves of her back, slid under her to cup her breasts.

His fingers barely brushed the sensitive tips, but it was enough to bring them surging to life. His lips were warm against the throbbing chord at the side of her neck, his teeth nipping delicately at the tautened flesh until she uttered a low moan of pleasure.

When she felt his body stiffen against her, she could have quite cheerfully throttled herself. She knew by the careful way he turned her onto her back that he had misinterpreted her strangled cry as one of pain.

A rueful grin lighted his face as he raised the covers up to her chin.

"So much for good intentions! Serves me right for upsetting you in the first place, doesn't it?"

"Josh, I . . ."

"Hush," he whispered, the tip of his finger pressing against her mouth. "After a cold shower, I'll be as right as rain."

"Don't go," she whispered, struggling against the lethargy brought on by the medicine she had taken.

She could almost feel his indecision, but he turned with a muffled oath and headed for the door. The room was plunged into darkness.

"Josh?"

"Sleep the pain away, my darling."

With a defeated sigh she gave in to the need for rest, but her mind clung to the endearment.

Diana was floating in the pleasant sphere between waking and sleeping, fighting to return to full consciousness in order to concentrate on the wonderful sensations her body was experiencing.

"Wake up, sweetheart." A voice murmured in her ear, the words punctuated by tiny nibbling bites upon the lobe. "Come on, babe. I've waited long enough."

Shaking her head to try and clear it, she was relieved to find her headache nearly gone. She opened her eyes, and for just a moment was alarmed. The room was dark and shadowy, and the man bending over her did nothing to reassure her. Without thought, she put her hands out to prevent his tender exploration of her body.

"How do you feel?" His head lowered to place a kiss on her parted lips.

"I'm fine." She turned her face, suddenly flustered. "Thank you for taking care of me the way you did."

"I enjoyed it." His laughter was muffled against her throat. "But somehow I think both of us will get more satisfaction out of the second phase of treatment." His hands slid down over her breasts and stomach to reach lower, and as his touch seared the flesh of her thighs her body jerked in involuntary response.

"Josh, we can't!" Her hands clutched convulsively at

his shoulders. She felt confused and vulnerable, more vulnerable than she had ever been. She seemed to have lost much of her ability to resist her own longings, and it was this very weakness that was going to make the situation between Josh and herself unbearable!

"Why not?" he whispered against her throat. "You may not want marriage, honey, but you sure as hell want me!"

Yes, she wanted him! Although she knew it was wrong, that she should resist and fight the power he wielded over her emotions, a tiny voice deep inside urged her to cease struggling. As his hands moved with delicate precision against her skin the responsive movements of her body made her need of him all too obvious. She was lost in an uncontrollable blaze of passion, and she mindlessly urged him on.

Josh shifted his weight until he lay against the length of her body, and she moaned as his mouth and tongue caressed her breasts. The solidness of his stirring masculinity against her stomach excited her, and she wantonly moved against him.

"Baby, don't," he groaned, his mouth moving until his words were spilled against her throbbing throat.

With a smile she ignored his command. She wanted to make him lose his rigid control. Her hands rose to clasp his strong neck, and she forced his mouth upward to meet hers. She moved her tongue against his lips, feeling a sense of power when she felt his body shudder with excitement.

This kiss was unlike any other they had shared. He didn't force her, but only moved his mouth sensuously against the parted moistness of her own, silently encouraging her to take the initiative and explore his lips and tongue more fully.

They were both drawing in deep lungfuls of air in panting gasps. His hands moved to cup her face as he tore his mouth away from hers. She moaned in protest and looked into his face reproachfully. Josh stared down into amber eyes that blazed honey-gold with arousal.

"God, you're driving me crazy, woman," he groaned. "I wanted to wait, but I can't . . . I can't!"

With relentless force he took what he wanted, his shivering frame lying against her moistened flesh only when he found the resting place he sought. For a moment he was still, and she blushed at the satisfaction in his eyes when a shiver of pleasure caused her to quake against him.

He lifted his upper body so that he could watch her face. A sensuous smile curved his lips as he began moving his hips in a slow spiral of seduction, which gave her exquisite pleasure and which she sought to intensify by the increasingly frantic arching of her hips.

"Slowly, honey," he murmured, stilling her with his hands. "There's no need to rush."

His mouth again explored the welcoming moistness of hers, and she was thrilled by the responses of her body to his skilled touch. But when she came close to reaching the apex of pleasure she sought, Josh would delay the final moment.

Although she knew he had her satisfaction as well as his own in mind, she resented the delay, her body demanding the inevitable conclusion of their embrace.

But she couldn't find the breath to protest as she writhed beneath his restrictive hold.

He was deaf to her urgings as he studied her face with rapt concentration. She was so lovely, he thought, his breath a tortured rasp in his chest.

As he stared in growing delight at the sensuous, giving woman in his arms he knew that nothing in life had ever prepared him for her. Never had he imagined the depth of need loving her was wrenching from his trembling body. For him she was the light dispelling the darkness of the past, and in that moment he knew that if he lost her, he would be forever blinded by the shadows.

Dear God, make her love me, he pleaded silently, his body moving passionately against her. He was rewarded by her cry of completion as she sobbed his name aloud, and he reached his own peak almost simultaneously. His only desire as wave after wave of shattering sensation engulfed him was to hold her and never let her go.

During the long hours of the night he reached for her again and again. He was thirsty, and slaked himself at her mouth. He was hungry, and satisfied himself with her body.

For Diana this was another dream out of time, and she never wanted to awaken to face a bitterly cold reality. She responded to him, giving herself up entirely into his skilled hands. She forgot her uncertainty over their relationship, forgot everything but the feel of him against her body, allowing the taste and scent of him to permeate her whole being. This time there was no holding back even a small part of herself, and she gloried in the giving as she strove with her hands and mouth to imprint herself forever on his willing flesh.

Josh hadn't given any more thought to setting the alarm than she had, and it was only the strident ringing of the hallway phone that penetrated the deep sleep they had fallen into during the early hours. Even as she wrapped the comforter from the foot of the bed around her goose-pimpled flesh and ran to answer it, she could hear him stumbling around the room in search of his clothes.

The caller was Ann, although it was difficult to recognize her voice. Harsh, raspy breathing punctuated by frequent coughing told its own story, and when she started to explain why she wouldn't be able to bring Steven to the school as early as she had promised, Diana cut her short.

"Don't be ridiculous. You stay in bed, and don't you dare move until I get there."

"Diana, there's no reason for you to drive this far out of your way. Bob's getting ready to take me to the doctor, and we can drop Steven off on our way."

"What time is your appointment?"

"I'm going as a drop-in. I was in the hospital a couple of months ago with pneumonia, but honestly, Bob's overreacting to this whole situation. I'm not as sick as I sound."

Since her protest was punctuated with grating coughs, Diana doubted the truth of the words. Checking the time on the clock visible through the arched opening into the living room, she came to a decision. Elaine wouldn't mind leaving a few minutes early to open the school, and if Diana hurried, she should have enough time to reach Ann and Bob's before they had to leave for the doctor's.

She outlined her plans to Ann, and although she insisted she was perfectly able to get all three boys dressed and fed, Diana sensed a note of relief in her voice.

"You're a darling, but you don't have to bother taking my two to school."

"It will save you time and energy, and I'll enjoy the drive. That is"—she hesitated—"as long as you trust me to take them."

"Now who's being ridiculous?" Ann snorted her disdain.

As soon as Diana ended the call she hurriedly dialed Elaine's number. As she had expected, Elaine was full of sympathy and told her not to worry about what time she arrived at school. "I can take care of the new admissions, and don't forget that Betty asked to switch her hours for today so she could attend a parent-teacher conference at her daughter's school during the afternoon. I'll have plenty of help settling the newest youngsters in."

"Thanks, Elaine. I'll try to get there before Betty has to leave." Laughter punctuated her voice. "Hopefully by that time, the screaming and crying for Mommy will have subsided somewhat."

"Humph," Elaine snorted. "I knew you had an ulterior motive."

She was just in the process of putting the receiver back in its cradle when Josh's voice roared. "Where the hell are my pants?"

She dropped the phone with a thud and hurried into the bedroom. A brief glance around the room showed no sign of the missing clothing, and she noticed Josh's exasperated expression with growing amusement.

"You're laughing at me again, woman!" Dressed only in snugly fitting shorts and his well-wrinkled shirt, he approached with mock ferociousness. Giggling, she neatly sidestepped his groping hands.

"Have you looked in the bathroom?"

Hitting his forehead with the palm of his hand, he strode past her, and she used the opportunity to slip out of the comforter and into her robe.

"Josh, will you hurry up in there? I've got to shower!"

The door opened abruptly, and she stumbled against him.

"Just be glad I'm a gentleman. I'll even fix breakfast while you make yourself beautiful for me."

"Some gentleman!" She peered at him through her lashes. "You not only monopolize my bathroom, but you probably used all the hot water to boot!"

"Not guilty." He grinned. He set her aside and finished buttoning his shirt. "If a five-minute wash uses up all the hot, then remind me to buy you a new water heater."

"Will you get out of here, before I throw something at you?"

"As long as it isn't those delectable panties you fling at my head, you're safe." His mouth curved in a definite leer, and she had to bite down hard on her lip to prevent giving in to threatened laughter. "In case you haven't noticed, I've got a thing about a certain part of your anatomy."

She managed to slam the door in his face before he could enjoy her chagrin. Recalling how often during the night his hands had squeezed and fondled the area in question, she felt a blush burning all the way from her toes to the top of her head. As she stepped into the shower, a sensual smile curved her mouth.

Diana bathed and dressed with record speed and within fifteen minutes had joined Josh in the kitchen. There had been some difficulty locating her brush, which she finally found kicked under the bed, and by that time she decided to forgo style and settle for just unruffling the tangles. With her hair falling around her shoulders and only a rich moisture cream smoothed into her skin, she looked vividly alive to the man who turned to greet her.

"Grab a chair." He smiled. "This morning I'm relieving you of your womanly duties."

Seating herself, she snorted inelegantly. "Cooking's no more a woman's job than driving a car is a man's. We can do anything you can do, and probably better. Women use brain instead of brawn. Why, someday we might not nee. men around at all!"

Josh's grin widened as he straddled the chair across from her. "After last night, that remark was unworthy of you, sweetheart."

At that point, Diana found the scrambled eggs and toast on her plate of sufficient interest to demand her undivided attention. They ate in companionable silence, until she sighed her satisfaction and moved to pour them both another cup of coffee.

"Diana?"

"Mmmm?"

"I love you."

His statement was made in such a dispassionate tone of voice that she thought for a moment she hadn't heard him correctly. For a startled instant her eyes lifted to his, and the tender demand she saw in his gaze almost completely unnerved her. Glancing down at the slow puddle of dark liquid staining the Formica tabletop, she returned the pot to the stove and grabbed a rag to wipe up the mess spreading beside Josh's cup.

After returning the rag to the sink, she had to force herself to turn around and face him. Those three simple words had stabbed to the heart of her, and she almost hated him for causing her so much confusion and pain. Why should he speak when there was no meaning behind what he said, when she knew even better than he did that his love held a false, empty promise?

"Did you hear what I said?"

"I heard." She couldn't help the callous abruptness of her response. The declaration of love that she had longed to hear had been uttered, but it meant nothing. She didn't believe him, even though she desperately wanted to. She resented the note of quiet insistence in his voice as he demanded a response, almost as much as she hated the way his eyes seemed to be trying to pierce her defenses.

She refused to let him see how weakened she was by his declaration, and she was weakened, she realized. Even during the height of their lovemaking, he had never once told her he loved her. He must have known the impact his words would have if he spoke them when she least expected them.

The more she thought about his systematic wearing down of her defenses, both in bed and out, the angrier she became. The migraine of last night had disappeared, and she had awakened this morning feeling both physical satisfaction and an inner warmth caused by his care of her. Now, though, she saw his concern as a ploy to gain his own advantage, and she was sickened by the knowledge that even knowing how she felt about marriage, he was determined to make her yield.

"Diana, look at me!"

Mutinously she did as he requested, lifting her head until she stared unblinkingly into his eyes. Tension built between them, but she refused to give in to the appeal she saw in his expression. She knew he was waiting for her to respond to words of love she knew to be false, but he could wait forever.

If she once lowered her defenses, she would be forever lost to herself, and that must never happen. If it did, there would be no victor. If there were just herself, she might risk a lifetime of regret, but she had to consider Steven. He would be caught between them, trapped in a loveless household.

If she married Josh, Diana feared that her own insecurities would work against their marriage, until even the friendship they had found together was destroyed. No! Steven's future, as well as her own, couldn't be risked until she was sure in her own mind that marriage between herself and Josh was the best for all of them.

"Oh, Josh!" She lifted a shaking hand to brush the hair from her face, while her shoulders slumped in dejection. "Please! Not now. I don't have the time this morning to get into a heavy discussion."

"Then damn it, we'll make the time! Do you honestly think we can go on this way?"

Diana just stared at him, and the very intensity of her look caused him to whiten until the bones of his jaw stood out in stark prominence.

"Diana?"

She shook her head, her movements slow and deliberate. "You're right," she whispered, ignoring the tears filling her eyes. "You can't accept our relationship the way it is, and I can't accept anything else. That doesn't leave us an alternative, does it, Josh?"

He rose to his feet, his fists clenched at his sides. She heard the rasp of his breath drawn deeply into his lungs and noticed the compression of his mouth with a curious sense of inevitability. Although she wanted to scream aloud her agony at the step she was taking, she knew it was the only way.

"I want to go back, Josh."

"What do you mean?"

"I'm talking about sharing Steven amicably between us, without complicating the situation by being anything other than friends." She saw his eyes briefly flare with emotion before he averted his head and walked toward the back door. His hand was on the knob, his knuckles whitening as his fingers exerted pressure.

"Please, can't we be friends, Josh?"

He turned to face her, and she nearly cried out at the agony that twisted his features. She wanted to go to him then, to wipe away the pain of her rejection, but even as she took a trembling step forward the bitterness of his words halted her.

"Do you think if it were possible to go back and live life differently, I wouldn't have done so before now?" His laughter was harsh. "Dear God! The things I would change if I had the chance!"

10

Diana couldn't stand his scrutiny a moment longer. Turning her back to him, she moved toward the sink and gripped the edge of the counter for support. It isn't fair, she thought, staring out of the window even as her sight turned inward. She had already risked too much of herself by loving the silent man behind her. As far as Josh was concerned, there was only one solution to the problem, but she didn't see it that way.

She had asked for so little, she decided, fighting down tears of self-pity. She'd tried to settle for the crumbs of his affection, knowing he still loved Joanna, but she had only been lying to herself. At the thought of her sister, new resolve tightened her lips. No! she vowed silently. Feeling the way she did, she knew it wouldn't be long before she demanded more than Josh could give, and then she would despise him as much as she was beginning to despise herself.

"I'm not going to marry you!" Her voice was flat, unemotional. I sound like I don't even care, she thought, knowing how far that was from the truth. Her words were simply a cover-up for her feelings, which were tearing her apart inside.

"For heaven's sake, what are you trying to do to me, Diana? Does it give you satisfaction to see me bleed, is that it? Are you using me to get back at all men, because one man was stupid enough to prefer Joanna to you?"

She whirled around, her eyes wide in the paleness of her face. "That's not true," she gasped, shaking her head in denial. "Coming from another man who preferred my sister, your accusation is ludicrous."

Josh braced himself against the doorframe, his eyes holding hers across the distance that separated them. "What I once felt for Joanna has no bearing on our relationship."

His quiet tones lent his words a sincere dignity that caught at her heart. How easy it would be to let herself believe him now, only to bitterly regret giving him her trust when the day came, as it surely would, when the agonizing pattern would begin all over again.

She recalled a particularly vivid memory of her childhood. She had made her parents a clay ashtray as a school crafts project and on Christmas morning waited breathlessly for her mother to finish unwrapping the gift. Even now she could almost feel the way her heart thumped against her chest.

"Darling, how lovely," her mother had cried, turning

to hug her younger daughter. "You must have spent hours making it for us. Why, I remember that darling little vase Joanna brought home when she was just your age."

Her laughter surrounded Diana. "She complained of working her fingers to the bone to have it ready for our anniversary, but we knew the angel didn't really begrudge the time. Do you remember how perfect it was, Herbert?" she asked, turning to her husband. "You were sure Joanna would grow up to be a sculptor."

Herbert Moreland nodded, his eyes meeting his wife's in remembered pleasure. "I guess I must have shown that vase to every man in the office!"

Diana could have reminded them of the day Joanna grabbed the small object from the mantel and shattered it against the wall during a temper tantrum, but she didn't bother. Her own offering lay forgotten, buried under the paper she had wrapped it in so lovingly. It never earned pride of place on the mantel, she remembered, and her father hadn't bothered showing it to his friends.

"Damn it, Diana!" Josh reached her in two lengthy strides, his hands gripping her shoulders. "Don't shut me out."

"You're not the one being shut out, Josh. Don't you understand? It's easy for you to say you no longer prefer my sister, but I could never believe you. The worst part of it is, I wouldn't even be able to blame you. But I have needs too, Josh, and I couldn't live forever in her shadow."

"You're nothing like Joanna."

"Don't you think I know that by now?" She shook her head, deliberately hardening lips that trembled. "Maybe if I hadn't superficially resembled her, I would have had a chance to develop my own personality. As it was, I spent my whole life apologizing for not being as bright and beautiful as she was. Whenever Joanna was away from home, I felt used as a means to keep her presence alive in a dead house. Well, I won't step into her shoes again, Josh, even for you. For me, being your wife would be both heaven and hell, because I'd know that if somehow Joanna could walk through the door, you would turn to her as if I didn't exist."

"That's not true!"

His hands slid across her shoulders until they rested against her neck. Gently his thumbs tilted her chin, until she could no longer avoid the eyes that inspected her features, one by one. She wanted to cringe from that glance; to hide herself from the comparison she had known to be inevitable.

"You little fool," he muttered, gripping the hair at her nape. He wanted to tell her that Joanna used her body as a weapon until a man was besotted enough to give her what she wanted, but he stopped himself from uttering the denigrating words. It went against the grain to speak ill of a woman who could no longer defend herself, especially to her own sister. Instead, he satisfied himself by muttering, "By the time you fell asleep in my arms, you had satisfied both my body and my mind, making me forget everything and everybody else, including Joanna."

As Diana remained silent, a growing feeling of helplessness nearly stopped his breath, bringing anger in its wake. An image of Joanna rose to his mind like bile in his throat, and he wanted to rip her memory from his thoughts. For nearly three years she had slowly and systematically stripped him of every shred of what passed for love between them. Diana only imagined a heaven and a hell, but he had lived it!

Strangely enough, the comparisons Diana feared had already been made, but it was Joanna who had come off the loser. How could he convince Diana of his love without causing her more hurt than she had already suffered? Would she even believe him? If she herself hadn't idolized Joanna, she wouldn't have spent her life trying to emulate her, and with a sense of hopelessness, he knew that he loved her too much to shatter her illusions about the sister she had lost.

He released her and began to move in the direction of the open doorway. "Nothing I do or say is going to make you believe that I love you. I'm tired of trying to prove myself to someone who uses her fear of the future as a weapon against me. The next step must be yours, Diana. My agent has been asking me to fly to Los Angeles to meet with the producer filming my latest book, and I think it's time I went. If I can get a flight, I'll leave in the morning. When I return, I promise I'll ask nothing more of you than the impersonal friendship you want. But somehow, I don't think a sterile relationship is going to satisfy us for long. You were made to be loved, and nothing you do will erase the memory of the nights we've shared together."

"Please . . . try to understand!" Her choked words held a fear she was too confused to acknowledge.

"I'm trying, but you're not making it easy for me, are you?"

She stubbornly remained silent, although to deny him meant denying herself. The emotional lid she had placed around her feelings remained inviolate, and without another word he walked from the room.

When she heard the thud of the door closing, she started to run after him; she was halfway across the floor before she stopped. No! It was better to make a clean break, to end it now before there was more hurt on both sides. Slowly she retraced her steps to the kitchen window, her eyes straining to catch a last glimpse of him. While she watched him round the corner of the house and disappear from sight, she stoically told herself that someday she would no longer hurt.

Again and again throughout the following days, Diana went over her last conversation with Josh. It wasn't as if she weren't busy . . . far from it. When Ann adamantly refused to follow the doctor's advice and enter the hospital, Bob had been at his wit's end wondering how he was going to keep her in bed until Diana insisted she come every evening to help.

Between fixing meals, caring for both Ann and the boys, and working during the day at school, she fell into bed pleasantly exhausted at night. But still her mind refused to give her any peace, and Josh was never far from her thoughts.

By the time she locked up the school on Friday, she was calm. She missed Josh more than she had believed possible and was beginning to feel that he was worth having at any price. Her love for him, whether or not it was returned, was the only thing in life that mattered anymore, the one thing she felt sure she would carry with her through death and beyond.

As she drove to Ann and Bob's she tried to keep her mind on the scenery flying past the car window but found herself once again thinking of Josh.

How could Joanna have left him? she wondered, until she remembered that as a child, Joanna had always discarded the toys that were no longer new and shiny. Had she dispensed with Josh in the same manner? When the newness wore off of their relationship, had she thrown away the love he felt for her, leaving him forever hungry for what he had lost?

She parked in front of the house by the lake, her face contorted with pain. She sat for a moment before getting out of the car and fought for composure. She was only thankful that Elaine had taken Steven home with her to spend the night. In his own way the little boy missed his father as much as she did, and in her present mood another question about when Daddy would be home would send her right around the bend.

Other than a slightly haunted darkness deep within her eyes, there didn't appear to be any physical signs of her inner turmoil. Ann might appear flighty and slightly scatterbrained, but Diana knew that her new friend had an uncanny knack of seeing what lay below the surface, and at the moment she just wasn't prepared to discuss Josh with any degree of composure.

After dinner, Diana insisted that Ann take a short nap. While she was sleeping, Bob and the boys helped

Diana clean the house and do the laundry, which had piled up during the last few days. The three males were surprisingly helpful, she admitted with inner amusement, as long as they were constantly told what to do. When they finished the last project she organized and just stood in the middle of the floor looking bewildered, she couldn't hold back any longer. They joined in her laughter, which awakened Ann, and soon they were all laughing.

That evening was the most pleasant she had spent in days. They sat around the living room eating popcorn and watching an old John Wayne western on television. The movie, a typical shoot-'em-up that delighted the boys, still had enough sweet romance in it to have Bob hooting, while she and Ann alternately giggled and glared at him.

It was late by the time the film ended, and Bob and Ann encouraged her to spend the night in the guest bedroom, but she refused, using the household chores neglected over the last few days as an excuse.

When Bob protested, Ann stopped him with a smile. "We can't keep her forever, honey. I'm nearly well, thanks to Diana, and if I flake out on you this weekend, you can play housewife."

"That's just what I'm afraid of." He groaned, tweaking the end of her nose. "Oh, well." He grimaced, his eyes twinkling. "Just lead and I'll follow, woman!"

Bob saw Diana to her car, Ann protesting vociferously when she was ordered to stay inside the house and out of the night air. They were still laughing when Diana attempted to start the engine, with no effect. Again she turned the key in the ignition, but only a small clicking sound resulted.

"Dead battery, by the sound of it."

She listened to Bob's pronouncement with exasperation. "Bob, I'm really anxious to get home. I hate to ask you, but . . ."

"After all you've done for us this last week, running you to your place is the least I can do. Just wait a minute while I tell Ann."

Bob made the trip in record time, obviously anxious to return to his wife. In the darkness of the car's interior Diana allowed herself a small smile of understanding. The two of them, Bob and Ann, had been sending signals to each other all evening, and she lost count of the times Ann mentioned how wonderful she felt. Remembering how often they had used any excuse to touch each other, she grinned.

At the time, she had been too busy to think much about the love and warmth her friends so obviously shared. Now she realized that her time with them had taught her an invaluable lesson. Diana recalled scolding Ann when Ann had become irritated with what she called Bob's "fussing."

Ann only giggled unrepentantly. "If I stopped complaining, Bob would think I didn't love him anymore, Diana. When you live with a man for as many years as I have, you begin to know his needs as well as your own. If you think I'm ornery, you should come over when Bob's off-color!"

Had that been the turning point in her thoughts about marriage to Josh? she wondered, or had loneliness already brought her to the realization that she needed him as much as she needed air to breathe. She had gone from fearing a future with him to dreading one without him, and she finally began to understand Josh's desire for a marriage to cement their relationship.

Neither of them could be satisfied for long with the impermanence of being lovers, and the thought brought with it a tremendous sense of release from the past.

Diana had been silent since she had entered the car. Finally, Bob turned his head to give her an encouraging smile. "Do you want to tell old Bob what's bothering you, honey?"

Her mouth twisting in the semblance of a grin, she shook her head. "Am I that transparent?"

"Not to me," he admitted, chuckling, "but you know that wife of mine by now. The last thing she told me as I walked out the door was to ask if there was anything we could do."

Diana bit her lip. She wanted to discuss her problems with the understanding man at her side. Yet the very fact that he had known Joanna, had been friends with Josh during the time he had been married to her sister, prevented her from questioning him. Somehow it smacked of disloyalty to Joanna, as if she were intruding on a relationship that was none of her business.

"Do you know how badly Josh needs you to love him, Diana?"

She stared at Bob, arrested by the solemn insistence in his voice.

"What has he told you?"

After negotiating a corner, Bob slanted a measuring look in her direction. Apparently satisfied with his inspection of her features, he began talking. He explained the reasons for the long estrangement between himself and Josh, giving Diana an insight into Josh's marriage that she had never had.

"Oh, Bob! Why didn't Josh tell me how miserable Joanna had made his marriage? Why did he let me go on thinking I was only a substitute for the woman he had loved?"

"She was your sister, Diana. Josh wanted to protect you from learning the truth about Joanna."

By the time Bob turned the car into her driveway, Diana was filled with hope. A blazing warmth enveloped her as her thoughts revolved around the man she loved so desperately. She thought of Josh's patience and understanding of her feelings, and she felt ashamed of the way she had rejected the love he offered her. And he did love her! He must if he risked his own chance at happiness by refusing to say a word against the sister he knew she loved.

Suddenly Diana knew what she must do. She would go to Josh in Los Angeles. She couldn't wait for him to return. He had told her the next step must be hers, and she wouldn't waste another minute.

Josh had been right all along, she realized. Because of her shattered relationship with Gilbert, she had used Joanna as an excuse to avoid becoming involved in another relationship that might hurt her. There was no guarantee for the future when two people tried to make a life together, but at least with herself and Josh, they could begin with honesty as well as love between them.

Bob left the motor running, and when he saw her to her door, she hugged him with exuberance.

"Thank you, Bob, from the bottom of my heart."

"Thank you, love," he said, returning her embrace with hearty enthusiasm before hurrying toward the car. "See you soon."

Diana felt absurdly happy as she rushed around, completing necessary tasks. In record time she had packed and arranged for Steven to remain with Elaine for a few days. Elaine, of course, was overjoyed with Diana's decision, calling her every kind of fool for waiting so long to admit she loved Josh.

While she waited for a taxi to arrive to take her to the airport, she paced the floor, irritated at the delay. If only she had her car, she thought, she could have been halfway to the airport by now. But if she had driven herself home, she would never have found out the truth from Bob! Then where would you be, stupid? she chided herself, jumping from sheer nervousness as a knock sounded at the door.

The impersonal smile for the taxi driver turned to one of joy when she saw Josh's large frame filling the doorway. With a stammered cry of welcome, she motioned him into the house, feeling ridiculously shy now that she was actually facing him. With jerky footsteps she moved toward the fireplace before turning to finally confess to him the love she had denied so long.

To her distress, the words froze in her throat as she stared at him. His warmly welcoming smile of only moments ago was gone, and in its place was an expression that was harsh with strain. His features whitened alarmingly as he glanced from her to the suitcase resting by the door.

"Josh, I . . . I didn't know you'd be coming home tonight. Why didn't you let me know?"

"I tried calling you from Los Angeles, but you weren't at home. Or were you simply not answering your phone?"

"Why would I do that?"

For long moments he was quiet, simply staring at her with a bleak gaze that confused her. The silence stretched unbearably until he turned with a muffled exclamation and removed his suit jacket. After throwing it carelessly over the back of the couch, he began loosening his tie, his hands pulling impatiently at the folds of silk as he slowly moved in her direction.

"I can think of one good reason, honey." He gestured to the full case, his eyes accusing as they returned to scrutinize her features. "Just for the record, were you even planning on letting me know your whereabouts, or were you just going to disappear, the way Joanna did?"

"Just what are you accusing me of?" she whispered, her face drained of all color as he moved even closer.

"I think that's obvious, don't you?"

She was numb with shock and didn't protest when his arms reached out to enfold her. Slowly his hands began a sensual exploration of her back, his palms sliding over her skin rhythmically.

"Little witch," he muttered hoarsely against the sensitive flesh of her neck, while his hands moved farther down her back to cup her curving softness and arch her against him. "Did you think I'd let you go so easily? Oh, God! I hate myself, but I can't let you leave me, Diana. Without you, life simply wouldn't have any meaning. Don't you understand? When Joanna left me, she nearly destroyed my pride, but you . . . you'll destroy *me!*"

The anger she had begun to feel at his suspicions melted when she saw the agony in his eyes. Slowly she turned, lifted the receiver from its cradle and dialed the number of the taxi service. After canceling her earlier request for a taxi, she again dialed the phone. Her eyes never leaving his, she clearly and precisely informed the travel agent that she was no longer interested in booking the first available flight to Los Angeles.

A flush darkened his cheeks as he realized the significance of her words. "Diana, I'm sorry," he whispered. "When I saw that damn suitcase, it was as if it were happening all over again, and I think I went a little crazy."

"I know what you thought. What I don't understand is why, Josh? How could you even for a moment think that I might leave you without a word of explanation?"

It all came out then, all the hurt and disillusionment he had felt toward his wife. "When I returned home from a disappointing meeting with an agent who I was hoping would represent me, I found her packed and ready to leave. I blamed myself for failing to make her happy and tried to reason with her, to get her to give our marriage another chance," he admitted tiredly, seating himself on the couch and cradling his head in his hands. "She was making a mess out of her life, but it wasn't entirely her fault. She had long ago sensed how tired I was of trying to keep a dead love alive, of forcing myself to fake a passion I no longer felt."

Diana cringed at the sound of laughter that held no amusement. "When I found out about Steven I couldn't wait to see him. I had wanted children desperately, and yet it took me weeks to get up enough courage to call you. I bought the condominium and then wasted even more time furnishing it, telling myself all the while that I wanted to provide my son with a home. The truth was, I was afraid of how I would feel when I saw you again."

"You had every right to despise me for what I did to you by keeping Steven's existence a secret."

"My fear about meeting you again had nothing to do with my son, Diana."

"What do you mean?" she whispered, her eyes holding his as desperation tautened her slender frame. Could she be mistaken, or was the emotion darkening his eyes familiar to her? Hadn't he looked at her in just that way the day they had met?

"I think you know, just as Joanna did. God help me, but from the moment I first saw you, I began resisting the hold she had on me. Your warm, loving eyes haunted me. She became the dreamy shadow of the past, while you became the reality. Can you understand why I've never been able to explain, why I've hidden my true feelings from you for so long? I fell in love with you the moment we met, although for a long time I tried to hide the truth from myself. But Joanna knew, and she couldn't live with the knowledge. She was selfish and shallow, but in her own way she loved me. That's why she was so jealous of you. When I discovered Steven's existence, I was overjoyed. But then the guilt began to eat at me, and I blamed myself for the way Joanna had died."

"Oh, Josh." She gasped. "You can't punish yourself like this. You did everything you could to save your marriage."

He nodded, but she could sense the doubt in him as clearly as if he had screamed it aloud. There was a haunted look in his eyes, and with a gasp Diana remembered another face, another time. She curled her fingers against her palms, feeling again Joanna's dampened flesh as she smoothed the hair from cheeks as white as the sheets on the hospital bed.

"Diana, I'm so scared!"

Her voice barely audible, Joanna had clutched at Diana's hand. As she had looked down at those clawlike fingers, which held so little strength, a sob had torn itself past the constriction in Diana's throat.

"I'm here, love," she consoled, seating herself on the side of the bed, her slight weight barely depressing the hard mattress. "You're going to be all right. Just fight back, Joanna. You've got to try!"

The trembling laugh Joanna uttered tore at Diana's heart. There was hysteria in the sound, but what really frightened her was the note of apathetic acceptance in her sister's voice. For some reason Joanna was allowing her life to just slip away, and she had to stop her. She had to!

"You have to live for your son, if not for yourself. He needs you, Joanna. The doctor's as worried as I am. I know you had a rough delivery, but during the last two days your condition has worsened, and there's no medical reason for it. You've got to try to overcome your depression. Please." She groaned, anguished tears soaking the pillow as she laid her head next to her sister, her arms circling the frail body with convulsive grief. "I can't lose you!"

"No matter how I've treated you in the past, I always knew you loved me," Joanna said, turning her head and studying Diana's ravaged features almost dispassionately.

"You're my sister!"

"Yes," she murmured, a wry smile curving her nearly bloodless lips. "But that never stopped me from hating you."

Diana winced, but her arms only tightened around Joanna. "I know," she whispered. She lifted her head and searched her sister's eyes to try to discover a spark of the affection for which she had always hungered.

At first she thought that even now, with Joanna clinging to her in trembling desperation, she would be disappointed. The eyes once so vivid and brimming with life were dimmed, the gaze turned inward. Selfish, greedy eyes that had only seen the younger sister who loved her as a threat. But now Diana saw the hard eyes softened by tears.

"Forgive me, Diana."

"Oh, Joanna." She gasped, lifting her against her breast and rocking her in her arms. "There's nothing to forgive any longer. Nothing!"

"I was so jealous of you!" The voice was weaker, a

wisp of breath hardly strong enough to feather lightly against Diana's throat. "Every time I hurt you, you only tried harder, and I hated myself as much as I hated you. You saw me as I was, and I couldn't stand it!"

"I thought you were perfect," she protested, loosening her hold until she could look into her sister's eyes.

"You were the perfect one. Oh, Diana! Why wasn't I able to feel the way you did? I've always thought only of what I wanted and needed. I don't think I've ever really cared about anyone else. You, Mom and Dad . . . Josh. It was an amusing game, to play one against another, but nothing more."

"That's not true!" Diana shook her head in repudiation at the callousness of Joanna's revelation. "Don't be so bitter toward yourself."

"It was true. Only, lying here, somehow things I've never cared about matter to me. I've done such terrible things, Diana. Such awful, hurtful things, and I deserve what's happened to me. I wish I could go back, and . . ."

"What, honey?"

Diana leaned closer, straining to hear Joanna's words. She felt closer to her sister than ever before and ached to retain the unfamiliar sense of kinship.

"The baby," Joanna murmured. "What does he look like?"

"He looks exactly like his mother, darling. He's so beautiful. Wait until you see him."

Joanna shuddered, a look of intense disappointment clouding her features. "Doesn't he look like Josh?"

Diana's voice was tinged with a resentment she found impossible to control. "He doesn't resemble Josh in the least." That animal! she had thought. It was his fault Joanna was unwilling to fight for a life that had ceased to be worth living. Maybe if she realized there was nothing in the child to remind her of a man she had every reason to hate, she might agree to at least hold the baby, just once.

"Oh, God! I'll never know for sure, will I?"

Throwing her head back against Diana's cradling arm, Joanna released harsh, mocking laughter. Her eyes shifted nervously, while straining fingers pleated the sheet.

Alarmed, Diana tried to soothe Joanna, but her words of comfort only seemed to worsen her sister's condition. Laying her back against the pillows, Diana rang for the nurse. She saw the red light go on above the bed with a feeling of relief, which was quickly stifled by the bruising pressure of Joanna's hand on her arm, a hand that only moments before hadn't contained enough strength to brush her own hair from her eyes.

"He mustn't ever know," she cried. "Promise me you'll never tell Josh about the baby."

Now, as she remembered giving that promise, the eyes she lowered toward Josh's bent head held stricken remorse. Slowly, she moved to stand in front of him. Placing gentle hands against his cheeks, she tilted his head until their eyes met.

"When she left you, was Joanna having an affair with another man?"

He winced, but didn't attempt to turn his head away. Slowly he nodded. "I wanted to spare you that knowledge," he muttered, his lips compressing. "How did you find out?"

"Just before she died, Joanna asked me what Steven looked like. I told her the truth, hoping she would be pleased that he didn't look like you. She became hysterical, talking of the terrible things she had done in her life to the people who cared about her. That's when she made me promise never to tell you about Steven. I thought she was afraid for the baby, but now, I believe that since she couldn't be sure you were really Steven's father, she wanted to protect you from enduring that final humiliation at her hands. In the end she was sorry for hurting you, Josh."

His eyes widened, quick tears forming behind the lids. With a sobbing groan he rested his head against her breast, shivering when her arms reached out to hold him protectively.

"Thank you," he muttered thickly. "Oh, Diana. I love you so much . . . so very much!"

As she realized the tremendous commitment Josh was making to her, her heart ached for the sister who had been too self-centered to appreciate the man she had married, until she lost him. Now she understood Joanna's insistence on blaming Josh for the failure of their marriage. She had needed to focus her hatred away from herself to survive, and compassion brought with it a final understanding.

"Just remember from now on that I'm not Joanna,

and trust me!" As she finally admitted the truth of her own words she felt the bonds that had fettered her to her sister snap. At last she was free of her shadow, and as her hand brushed soothingly against Josh's silvered hair, she again whispered, "I'm not Joanna!"

Slowly his head lifted, and glanced into moist eyes eloquent with pride . . . and pity. As if her compassion tortured him, his lids shut out the sight of her, his breath rasping through his heaving chest.

Kneeling beside him, she held him close and murmured words of love and comfort even as she ached from the strength of the arms that locked her against his chest. Her warmth released the restraint that had marred their relationship, and now the beauty of the things he whispered in her ear had no place in the past, and never would have.

"I'll make all this up to you, love," he whispered, nuzzling his mouth against her neck. His hands were smoothing her hair, as if he couldn't get enough of the feel of her. "I won't pressure you into a marriage you don't want. Just let me love you and Steven and take care of you both."

With joy bursting inside of her, she nearly laughed aloud at this new humbleness in the man she loved so deeply. Determined to shock him into his usual possessiveness, she murmured, "Of course, Josh. Although it'll be different when I marry, I suppose."

"Marry, hell." He growled, his eyes darkening. Glowering at her, he caught his breath as he read the amusement on her face. "You little witch, you're putting me on!"

She gurgled with laughter. "Don't you want me to marry you?"

His trembling fingers held wonder as they traced her features. "I don't deserve to have you. You know that, don't you?"

"Ummm, don't I just," she teased, linking her hands behind his neck and drawing his mouth nearer to hers. "If I thought there was any chance for escape, you wouldn't see me for dust. But since I adore you, and always will, I don't see any sense in running away, do you?"

As his mouth found hers and he felt the response of her parted lips, he forgot to be gentle. His kiss hardened and deepened abruptly until their hearts were pounding in unison. Swiftly his hands dispensed with their clothing, and as he began to lower her beside him on the couch she moaned, loving the feel of his fingers against her flesh.

"Don't stop me now." He groaned against her mouth, his body shaking.

As if she would try, she thought, her mind hazy with desire as his mouth trailed over the hidden places of her body until she was gasping. Writhing with ecstasy, she began her own hungry exploration of his flesh, and she delighted in his shuddering response.

"Yes." He gasped, half lifting his head to watch her. He grasped her head in his hands, holding the moment until he couldn't stand it any longer. With a strangled cry he struggled for control and quickly covered her body with his own.

It had been a long journey, but as Diana molded herself against him, Josh knew he had finally reached home. Even as he cried her name in a frenzy of pleasure, he felt the shadow of Joanna's betrayal receding, until he was left with only the peaceful aftermath of shared love.

YOU'LL BE SWEPT AWAY
WITH SILHOUETTE DESIRE

$1.75 each

1 ☐ CORPORATE AFFAIR
James

2 ☐ LOVE'S SILVER WEB
Monet

3 ☐ WISE FOLLY
Clay

4 ☐ KISS AND TELL
Carey

5 ☐ WHEN LAST WE LOVED
Baker

6 ☐ A FRENCHMAN'S KISS
Mallory

7 ☐ NOT EVEN FOR LOVE
St. Claire

8 ☐ MAKE NO PROMISES
Dee

9 ☐ MOMENT IN TIME
Simms

10 ☐ WHENEVER I LOVE YOU
Smith

$1.95 each

11 ☐ VELVET TOUCH
James

12 ☐ THE COWBOY AND THE
LADY   Palmer

13 ☐ COME BACK, MY LOVE
Wallace

14 ☐ BLANKET OF STARS
Valley

15 ☐ SWEET BONDAGE
Vernon

16 ☐ DREAM COME TRUE
Major

17 ☐ OF PASSION BORN
Simms

18 ☐ SECOND HARVEST
Ross

19 ☐ LOVER IN PURSUIT
James

20 ☐ KING OF DIAMONDS
Allison

21 ☐ LOVE INTHE CHINA SEA
Baker

22 ☐ BITTERSWEET IN BERN
Durant

23 ☐ CONSTANT STRANGER
Sunshine

24 ☐ SHARED MOMENTS
Baxter

25 ☐ RENAISSANCE MAN
James

26 ☐ SEPTEMBER MORNING
Palmer

27 ☐ ON WINGS OF NIGHT
Conrad

28 ☐ PASSIONATE JOURNEY
Lovan

29 ☐ ENCHANTED DESERT
Michelle

30 ☐ PAST FORGETTING
Lind

31 ☐ RECKLESS PASSION
James

32 ☐ YESTERDAY'S DREAMS
Clay

Silhouette Desire

Coming Next Month

Heart Over Mind by Sara Ann West

Brad Morrison was her boss and fiance, but Abby Kent found herself attracted to sculptor Travis Connery. Alone with Travis in New Mexico Abby was unable to resist his passionate persuasion.

A Wild, Sweet Magic by Suzanne Simms

He was too smooth, too rich, too handsome—the perfect target for cartoonist Kit Sinclair's wicked pen. But tycoon James Steele struck back, igniting a wild passion between them.

Experiment In Love by Rita Clay

Writer Victoria Brown was hoping to find a good story by advertising through a dating service. How could she know that Kurt Morgan had exactly the same idea?

Her Golden Eyes by Sara Chance

Tawny Summer McAllister was a born sailor, but from the moment Brandon Marshall stepped on board she was swept away by a wave of desire that engulfed them both.

Silver Promises by Suzanne Michelle

When TV newswoman Miranda Bowen met marine biologist Julian Hunter, she knew there was something special between them . . . something no ocean could keep apart.

Dream Of The West by Nora Powers

Melinda Adams was stunned when Cal, the rugged cowboy who had pursued her, turned out to be art collector Colin Marsden who remained aloof . . . with only his eyes betraying his desire.

Get 6 new
Silhouette Special Editions
every month
for a 15-day FREE trial!

Free Home Delivery, Free Previews, Free Bonus Books.
Silhouette Special Editions are a new kind of romance
novel. These are big, powerful stories that will capture
your imagination. They're longer, with fully developed
characters and intricate plots that will hold you spell-
bound from the first page to the very last.

Each month we will send you six exciting *new*
Silhouette Special Editions, just as soon as they are published. If you enjoy them as much as we think you will,
pay the invoice enclosed with your shipment. **They're
delivered right to your door with never a charge for
postage or handling, and there's no obligation to buy
anything at any time.** To start receiving Silhouette Special
Editions regularly, mail the coupon below today.

Silhouette Special Edition

READERS' COMMENTS ON SILHOUETTE DESIRES

"Thank you for Silhouette Desires. They are the best thing that has happened to the bookshelves in a long time."
—V.W.*, Knoxville, TN

"Silhouette Desires—wonderful, fantastic—the best romance around."
—H.T.*, Margate, N.J.

"As a writer as well as a reader of romantic fiction, I found DESIREs most refreshingly realistic—and definitely as magical as the love captured on their pages."
—C.M.*, Silver Lake, N.Y.

*names available on request